Honest
Doubt

Honest Doubt

AMANDA CROSS

BALLANTINE BOOKS • NEW YORK

A Ballantine Book
The Ballantine Publishing Group

Copyright © 2000 by Amanda Cross

www.randomhouse.com/BB/

Library of Congress Cataloging-in-Publication Data
Cross, Amanda, 1926–
Honest doubt / Amanda Cross.—1st ed.
p.   cm.
ISBN 0-345-44011-0
1. Fansler, Kate (Fictitious character)—Fiction. 2. Women private
investigators—United States—Fiction. I. Title.
PS3558.E4526 H66 2000
813'.54—dc21
00-041445

Manufactured in the United States of America

First Edition: December 2000

10   9   8   7   6   5   4   3   2   1

To my kin and kith
in Park Slope

There lives more faith in honest doubt
Believe me, than in half the creeds.
—Tennyson

Honest
Doubt

CHAPTER ONE

Some work of noble note, may yet be done.
                    —Tennyson, "Ulysses"

When I had finished writing up my report, covering everything in the investigation as it then stood, I leaned back in my chair and gave myself up to facing facts. So far, so good, but only so far and no further. I knew the moment had come to call upon Kate Fansler.

She had been recommended to me as the logical, perhaps the only, person who could be of help at the current impasse. As a private investigator of some reputation and accomplishment, I never shy away from consulting anyone who can offer me a shove, however minimal, in the right direction, but Kate Fansler gave me pause. She was a detective herself, if strictly amateur, and a professor into the bargain. I don't mind asking experts for explanations in any abstruse field—I'm ready to admit what's beyond my powers—but I couldn't help fearing that the air that lady breathed was a little too rarefied for my earthly self.

And then of course there was the fact that she was

said to be slender. I, being fat, dislike thin women—
I'm more open-minded about men—and in the end I
admitted this to my client, the one who had suggested
Fansler. I was guaranteed that though she was undoubt-
edly skinny—that term, being vaguely insulting, ap-
peals to me—Fansler never worried about her weight or
threatened to go on a diet.

If there is one thing more revolting than another, it is
thin women complaining about their fat and screaming
about their need to lose weight. Not Fansler, I was assured. With her it's a matter of metabolism—genes,
really. She eats what she wants and hates health food
and any form of low-fat diet, my client told me. Well,
blessings are unevenly distributed in this world, though
Hindus think we all earned our fate by our actions in a
previous life. I probably was starving, skeletal, and
yearning for food every minute of the day and night.
Hence my current figure.

I'd gone to many doctors and diet specialists, all of
whom tried to determine why I was fat, and how I
might get thin. It was always assumed it was some
problem with my psyche. One day I happened to meet
up with a doctor who explained that there was such a
thing as an inherited tendency to largeness. He held to
this view even under my vigorous cross-examination. I
began not only to accept the fact that I was fat, that my
father had weighed three hundred pounds and my

mother not far behind, but that, furthermore, once people got used to the idea of my size it might not matter that much anymore. It was genes with me, same as with Fansler.

But of course it still matters. I collect plump people who are accomplished as well as heavy. It helps to knit up my raveled self-esteem. People seldom realize it, but fat is the only affliction that has never been protected by affirmative action, antibias laws, or any other category like sexual harassment, date rape, or domestic violence, though I seem to remember someone once wrote a book called *Fat Is a Feminist Issue.* The point is, it's okay to say and do anything to fat people short of murder, and to refuse them a job because you think their failure to lose weight is a character and mental defect. They don't even call it heft-disadvantaged or weightily challenged.

There was Nero Wolfe. It's easier for men, of course, with this as with everything else. Dorothy Sayers was fat. When she lived in Witham, they used to say that her husband drank and she ate. When she wasn't translating Dante, that is. When she'd had enough of Peter Wimsey. I'm afraid I've gotten in the habit of mentioning my size to bring it out into the open when I meet someone so that we can go on to other things. I'd have to be careful not to overdo that with Kate Fansler.

Enough, I told myself firmly. Without thinking about it too much, I picked up the phone and called her, introducing myself as recommended to her by Claire Wiseman, who used to teach at Clifton.

"Ah," Fansler said, "what Charles Dickens called a mutual friend." She made an appointment to see me at her home the next afternoon.

My name is Estelle Aiden Woodhaven, licensed as a private investigator; everyone calls me Woody. Estelle was my grandmother's name; Aiden is what they would have named me if I'd been a boy, which they had rather hoped I would be. It's easy to figure out what Woody is short for; I think it definitely sounds investigative, which Estelle certainly does not. One of the fancy academic types I've been dealing with said it sounded androgynous, so people wouldn't know I was a woman until they were face-to-face with me. Right, I thought; and they wouldn't know I was fat, either.

Of course, I didn't say all this to Kate Fansler when I met her the next afternoon; I just drew attention to my size, because I find it's necessary to assure clients and those I consult that I may be fat, but I can get around. In fact, I told her, I coach a college hockey team—field hockey, not ice; I'm also trained in self-defense. Also, I pointed out, there's an advantage in looking like a lazy linebacker if you're not really sluggish.

"Sorry to have put you through all that," I said to

Kate Fansler. "I guess the thought of talking to you made me nervous."

Kate opened her mouth and closed it. She put on glasses to read the card I had handed her, which she had been too polite to look at while I was talking. Now she gazed at me over her glasses, which gave her the look of a psychoanalyst I'd once gone to, another thin dame, who had knitted throughout our sessions when she wasn't peering at me over her spectacles. She hadn't helped me at all, and neither had any of the other shrinks I'd been advised to consult.

"I didn't know anyone played field hockey anymore," Kate said. "We used to play it in school; I was a wing— much smacking of ankles with sticks."

"Not if it's played properly," I said with dignity.

"I shall come by one day and watch the team you coach," Kate said. "Meanwhile . . ."

"What am I here for? My usual tasks involve divorce, theft, blackmail, suspicions of commercial cheating. Now I've been hired for a job that's a bit beyond my scope; I was hoping to hire you as a consultant, a subcontractor, whatever. Is there a chance you might agree?"

"There's a chance I might listen. May I venture a guess that your case has to do with an academic or literary matter?"

"They said you were a good detective."

Kate smiled. "It hardly took detective powers to guess that. Tell me about it, and we'll see if I think I can help. Won't you sit down?" she said, waving toward a chair. I had been standing while I made my speeches and handed her my card. Now I sat.

"Can't I get you a cold drink?" Kate said. It was late September but really hot—Indian summer or something. Even though riding a motorbike is cooler than walking, you're still moving through the humidity and heat and likely to be sweating upon arrival. Not that a taxi would have been much better; they aren't really air-conditioned whatever they claim. The subway cars are cool enough, but the stations are Turkish baths.

"A glass of cold water would be welcome," I said. I seemed to take a lot of time deciding what to say to her. She left the room to fetch my drink, and I took the op-portunity to look around. I'm not much interested in furniture as a rule; I only notice it when it concerns some problem I'm trying to figure out. I'm good at noticing; any half-decent detective has to be good at noticing, but I don't sit around describing every-thing to myself the way they seem to do in books. This room was appealing, however, cool of course—there was an air conditioner—but also comfortable, as though they'd bought some pretty good furniture a while back and just let it grow old along with them. A bit shabby,

I guess it was, but you didn't get the feeling they were trying to impress anyone with their good taste. This was just a room to sit in.

Kate came back with a tall glass of water for me and one for her too. I drank mine eagerly, not caring how thirsty I looked. Kate sipped hers, which made me decide she brought herself a drink of water to make me feel comfortable. She seemed to me a nice sort of person, nothing special, but not hard to be with, which was all very fine, but the question was, Would she be willing to help me? The truth was, I didn't really see why she should bother, in this heat, with a backbreaker of a case that hadn't anything to do with her.

I'd put my glass down and was about to launch into my long history when something happened—a very small thing, really, but I think it somehow made a bond between us. I'd heard a door open and shut, and a man, who'd obviously just come in, walked past the living room, where we were sitting, without looking our way. Kate didn't say anything, so I didn't either, and then a huge dog appeared in the doorway. It just stood there, looking at us, and then wandered over to Kate to say hello.

I've got to admit I'm a nut about dogs. I've never had one; my parents thought they were just dirty beasts, not fit to be in a civilized house, and once I'd left home I couldn't take charge of any animal who was depending

upon me for the basics of life, not to mention company.
This great creature was a Saint Bernard. I leaned toward
the dog and held out my hand.

"Let me say hello to you," I addressed the dog, who
got up slowly, as that size dog does most things, and
moved over to inspect me. After letting myself be
sniffed in the proper way, I put my hands around that
great big head and cooed; well, that's what I did, I
cooed, calling him a magnificent and beautiful creature.
He sat down and put an enormous paw on my knee.

I told Kate about always wanting a dog. "He's wonderful," I said.

"It's a she," Kate said. "Banny is her name; it was her
name when we got her. Her former owner, who had
bred her, named all her puppies after actors: Anne Ban-
croft, in this case."

"Beautiful Banny," I said. To a non–dog lover I
would have sounded giddy, if not of questionable sanity,
but no owner of Banny could fail to understand my in-
fatuation. After a pause, to show no rejection was meant,
Banny left me to lie next to Kate Fansler. Somehow it
was easier to tell my story now.

"First of all," I began, still trying to put off the moment of actually starting to outline the case, "do you
know much about Tennyson?"

"The woman in the *Prime Suspect* series?" Kate asked.
"The one played by Helen Mirren? If I was naming

Banny after an actress now, I'd name her after Helen Mirren."

"Not Jane Tennison," I said, delighted with the response. "The poet Tennyson—Alfred, Lord. Victorian. I tried to read his poetry when this case came up, but it seemed awfully long-winded to me. I thought he could have said what he wanted to say a lot more simply in prose, but I don't really know anything about poetry."

"T. S. Eliot would have agreed with you," Kate said. "He didn't care for Tennyson's poetry, but he said one thing about Tennyson that I've always felt was also true of me. Eliot said that Tennyson was 'the most instinctive rebel against the society in which he was the most perfect conformist.' I've often been accused of the same thing."

"Are you a conformist?" I heard myself asking.

"Superficially, I suppose. I'm married, I don't have to worry about money, I value courtesy. I do, all the same, feel rebellious about much in our society. But you haven't come here to discuss me. How does the poet Tennyson come into it?"

"The professor who was murdered was a Victorian specialist and a particular admirer of Tennyson. In fact, he was writing a book about Tennyson when he died."

"Perhaps you'd better start at the beginning," Kate said. "I make no promises, but we can at least decide if I'm able to help."

"I didn't come in at the beginning," I said. "At first murder wasn't suspected, and he was buried in the small cemetery near his country home; you know the sort of thing, sweet grassy spots, with a huge tree shading them and the best view to be found for miles around; I saw it and I wouldn't mind lying there myself for all time. Fortunately, as it turned out, he was buried and not cremated, though I suppose it was no surprise, since he was remarkably old-fashioned in all his ways; he'd left strict instructions about the family plot, which he had bought some years ago. His wife had been buried there, though she had let her children know that she wished to be cremated, and was. One of the many things I learned in the course of this case was that ashes can be interred in a churchyard as well as a body."

"I'm to gather they had to dig him up to find the cause of death," Kate said, coming crisply to the point as was, I would soon learn, her habit.

"Exactly. His son came home when he, the father, died, and insisted there was something phony about the death. The dead man, the father, the professor—why don't I call him by his name, which was Charles Haycock—Charles had married again, rather soon after his wife's death, and none of his three children much cared for their stepmother, who was, and is, a rather selfish and bossy woman. Cynthia is her name. In addition to the son who raised the suspicion about his father's death and who is named Hallam—something to do with Tennyson, as I understand it—and has always been called Hal, there are his older brother, Charles Jr., called Chuck, and his younger sister, Maud, also a name with a Tennyson connection, or so I was informed. Can you possibly follow all this?"

"I think I've got it," Kate said. "Trying to set forth a whole case from the beginning is like trying to describe step by step how one puts on an overcoat—not easy. So son Hallam had Papa dug up?"

"After a great deal of rumpus, I was told. And they found the wrong drug in him, some pill that would be fatal to anyone with a weak heart, or for that matter anyone. I've got the names here, if you can hold on a minute."

"Let's get back to that later," Kate said. "Go on."

"Hallam immediately accused his stepmother, who inherits the father's house, pension, life insurance, and social security. She was, it turned out, far away on the day her husband died, but that seemed to Hallam less an alibi than evidence against her. After all, he kept saying, anyone can play hanky-panky with medications."

"Well, you certainly don't *need* to be present to poison someone," Kate said. "It's not like shooting them or stabbing them with a handy knife from the kitchen.

But if you're going to slip them something fatal, you probably need to be there to supervise the administration. I suppose one could mix the fatal dose in with some daily medication, but that's certainly chancy and might well be noticed by the guy taking it. Is this when you came in?"

"Yes, just about then. The police admitted they had a homicide on their hands, and the family—that is, the professor's children—were not satisfied with the progress the police were making, so they hired me. I was recommended to them by someone whose money had been cleverly diverted to the account of a con man and for whom I had recovered it, or most of it. Also, I think they supposed that a woman would be likelier to understand familial suspicions. I'd hardly begun on the case, and who knows where it would have ended, except that there came an anonymous letter. Well, almost anonymous. It was written on a computer and printed on the sort of machine available to, if not owned by, thousands of people, maybe millions. No clue there, except that the letter was written on English department stationery from Charles's college; it's called Clifton, by the way. It claimed that he had been murdered by a member of the department out of 'frustration and detestation and for political reasons'; I remember the wording exactly."

"So the police turned their attentions to the English department, which in turn called upon you," Kate suggested.

"That's more or less how it happened. Hal, the older son, still thought his stepmother could have sneaked into the department and written the letter to draw suspicion away from herself, but he agreed to let the department hire me in their turn to discover if their favorite suspect could have committed the crime. I wasn't that eager to take the job, frankly. The college is in New Jersey, which is a bit of a drag, and the police are from there and not that welcoming to private eyes, less so to women. The New York police have kind of gotten used to us."

"Did the whole department agree about hiring you?"

"Not the whole department, no. I think it was only one or two of them. The accusation seemed to be focused upon a woman in the department whom Charles had frustrated at every turn. I guess my being a woman helped here too; they thought I might understand the feelings of the suspect better than a man. And I didn't have to investigate the case all over again from the beginning, as a new detective would have been obliged to do."

"Let me guess," Kate said. "Charles was antifeminist, misogynistic, and generally the worst sort of old boy who devoutly wished women had never been admitted to higher education in the first place. It had been such a comfortable, chummy, male world before the female intrusion."

"You got it. I guess Claire Wiseman was right about your being the person who could help me with this case. She knew this other woman who'd formerly been in the department, and when she heard I was taking on the case, she suggested that I get in touch with you for stuff about academic departments that puzzled me. I'm afraid that's just about everything."

"If I can unravel the syntax, I may be able to help. Pronouns are the main problem; it takes a while for the listener to attach them to the right person. I've tried talking about cases to someone who didn't know the cast of characters, and I was always saying, not that one, the other one who . . . You're doing very well so far."

I heaved a great sigh and plunged in again. "Anyway, two men in the department had decided to hire me to find the murderer, before Claire heard about it. These two men are the only ones who can afford my price, though maybe there are other sympathizers. Investigating the family was right up my alley. But what do I know about English departments? Are they really likely to harbor a murderer, and is resenting female professors and graduate students a sane motive?"

"Yes to the first question," Kate said, "but they usually go about it in less physical ways: murdering the spirit, you might say. There was a case like that that I was involved in many years ago. Yes also to the second question; if any motive for murder can be considered sane, there are endless possibilities once you've eliminated relatives. Most murders happen between members of the family, so Hallam may turn out to be right after all. But academic departments are as likely to harbor a lunatic, or a fanatic, as are banks, law offices, the stock exchange, or anywhere else you can mention. I will admit, however, that most professors prefer less physical murder if it is available to them."

"Does that mean you think it was likelier to be the family, or that some professor may have been pushed too far?" I realized that a plaintive note had crept into my voice. "Not that you can decide on the basis of what I've told you so far; I do understand that. I just wondered what your first reactions were."

"To you or to the case?" Kate asked, her smile softening the directness of the question.

"Both, I guess. If we join forces, we can call ourselves Jack Sprat and wife. I do have trouble eating lean."

"Woody, listen to me. I'm not lean. Like everyone else my age, I'm dealing with gravity, which is to say one's body keeps migrating downward. I haven't gained weight, but the jeans I used to wear are now too tight for me over the butt, so I suggest we avoid comparisons. I don't mind your talking about your size, if it eases life for you, but I'd prefer not to discuss mine. Is it a bargain?"

"Not if you don't help me with the case," I said. "If you don't help, I'll turn up every other day on your doorstep and comment on your leanness. That's a threat and a promise."

"Okay, I'll help; you must have figured out by now that I'll help. Ordinarily I don't react kindly to this kind of request, but I can't resist the persuasions of fat people. Are we even now?"

"Even," I said.

"Here's the arrangement from my point of view," Kate said. "I'm not a subcontractor, or professional consultant, or any kind of authority with special knowledge. But if you would like to come and visit with Banny, since you've been so dog-deprived, she and I will welcome you, given advance notice of your arrival. Is that acceptable?"

"Yes," I said. "It is."

"Meanwhile," Kate went on, "if you would send me two lists, one of the Haycock family, and one of the English department at the college concerned, I'll try to get my facts straight. In fact, it would help if you could get me a catalog from the college, or a list of the classes to be taught next semester. I don't know the college and I ought to learn at least a little about it."

I walked over to say goodbye to Banny, who looked up and thumped her large tail against the floor. I thought to myself, She's big like a fat person; it's work to get up and easier to be agreeable from a reclining position. Besides, when you're big you have a sense of being in charge, no matter what is likely to occur. That was clearly how Banny felt, and I decided to feel that way too.

"Maybe you and I can take a walk with Banny when all this investigation is over," I said by way of farewell.

"We'll both look forward to it," Kate said. She got up and escorted me to the door. Banny stayed where she was. I would have liked to stay too, but one can't spend all day talking to professors and admiring large dogs, I firmly reminded myself.

When I got back to my office in Chelsea, once I had dealt with my messages and greeted Octavia, who worked for me as secretary part-time and, as far as I could see, studied law full-time, I allowed myself to sink into a kind of reverie about my visit to Kate Fansler. I am not, by nature, given to "processing" my experiences, to use what one of my clients told me was the term for playing over encounters in search of their meaning. Kate Fansler was an unusual person for me to meet in the line of duty, or outside of it, for that matter. I don't face quite as many physical dangers as women private eyes do in books, and I don't meet up with cases because some long-lost relative asks for my help, but I don't sneer at detective fiction the way some police people do. If books were as dull as most of my cases, no one would read them. I'm willing to do divorce, but it's not my favorite. It's a damn good cure, all the same, for dreams about happy marriage. It's amazing the hate people can develop for those they started out loving. And hate, as any detective or lawyer involved with divorce can tell you, is a lot more powerful than love, and much likelier to become an obsession.

Kate was married—I'd already learned that—and I supposed that the male figure marching past the living room was the man in question, but maybe they'd worked it out better than most. Ever since President Clinton's sexual escapades, I've been convinced, if I hadn't been before, that no one knows anything about a marriage except the people in it, and they only talk when hate takes over.

The odd thing about my meeting with Kate was that she didn't ask me how I became a private investigator. She's the only woman I ever met who didn't ask that question. They all seem to think there's some romantic story to be told, even by a fat woman, and they think the likelihood of being shot or beaten up is very high.

My experience with guys who try to wrestle or slug me to the ground is that they underestimate my fighting skills and are often not in great shape themselves— shape here referring to physical condition, not bodily contours.

I wondered why she didn't ask me the usual question. Because she had other ways of finding out, or because she didn't like personal questions and therefore avoided them, or what? I'd have been glad to tell her, but then I would have been glad to stay and talk about almost anything. One of the disadvantages of this job, which mostly suits me just fine, is that you never get to settle down and just chat with someone. When you've asked the necessary questions you get out, and feel lucky not to have been thrown out.

Claire Wiseman told me Kate's husband was a law professor and used to work in the D.A.'s office, so maybe she knew how people become private investigators, and didn't like to probe for my personal account. Lots of private eyes have been lawyers, so probably she knew how it went.

That's the way it went with me. I got out of law school with all the usual ideals, and moved to New York City, where I'd always wanted to be, and became a legal aid lawyer; they're called public defenders everywhere else, but it's the same everywhere. They're the ones who on no notice are provided as lawyers to the poor rats who can't afford a lawyer of their own. It's not a bad life. Sometimes you go to trial—I liked that best if there was a decent chance of getting your client off. For the most part, though, you had to realize you were just part of a system for flushing the poor, mostly black, criminals out of sight and out of mind. Still, I did some good, I liked it all right, I was good at it, good with the clients, good at litigation, able to get people to see that even though I was fat and not anybody's ideal, we all stood a chance. Something like that, anyway.

Then the mayor, Giuliani, it was—I never cared for him—took out after legal services. He got rid of a lot of administrators and supervisors who weren't pulling their weight, but he also bought out a lot of lawyers, including me. A guy I knew asked me if I'd like to establish a firm with him and another man, and I thought, Why not? I could still be called to defend the same people I'd defended in legal aid, make a decent living, and maybe get some other cases besides. What I discovered was that I really was a loner. Partners were okay—mine were nice enough guys—but I didn't like having to decide everything after long consultation. I'd hired some private investigators before and after I left legal aid, and the more I saw of them, the more I got the feeling that this was the life for me.

The two guys saw me go with mixed feelings—I think they were undecided about introducing me to some of their clients, and they were embarrassed when our clients always thought I was their secretary. They've stayed in touch. They even hire me from time to time and recommend me. By now I've got my own place—two rooms, and not grungy like the offices of Spenser or V. I. Warshawski. I like things to be orderly—not necessarily spick-and-span—but I like to know where my stuff is and how I can lay my hands on it.

I'd have liked to have told all this to Kate, maybe just to hear what she'd say, which is odd because mostly I'm bored to death explaining to people what I do and how I came to do it.

The phone rang, and Octavia buzzed through to say it was a client returning my call. I dragged myself out of "processing" my life and came back to living it. I told the caller that I had found the young man who had stolen stock from his store together with the cash in the machine. The kid, which he was, if not a juvenile, had also left the store unattended and unlocked. That the place hadn't been cleaned out was sheer good fortune—nobody had noticed that it was open to the world, and the owner had returned before any more harm was done. When he came to hire me, I told him that even if he caught the culprit, the merchandise would have been sold—it was unlikely anyone could get it back—and as for the cash, forget it. He said he knew all that, but he was angry and wanted the kid convicted. I could tell, talking to the man, that he had liked and trusted his employee and minded the betrayal of his affection more than the material loss. The kid hadn't covered his tracks at all.

I surmised, in fact, that he'd been talked into it by one of his buddies and wasn't unredeemable; but holding out a helping hand to kids from the inner city isn't possible, as I'd long ago learned in legal aid. I'd offer cigarettes, but there wasn't much point in offering anything more. They'd been living their desperate lives too long to welcome a helping hand, or to trust it. Well, so it goes. What could you do with a Congress that hated cities, New York most of all, and that got more credit voting money for a new bomber than for help to the inner cities, which, having been rendered hopeless by the politicians in government, were now blamed for being hopeless? It didn't seem to do anybody any good to think about it.

I decided to call it a day, and said goodbye to Octavia. She would take care of the bills, if any, send out my statements of payment due—I made my progress reports in person or by telephone—and close the office. I'd only been able to afford Octavia in the last year, but I made enough money to warrant it, and I found that having a secretary answer the phone, having an outer office with someone in it, makes a big impression on possible clients trying to estimate my capabilities.

Of course, having a secretary says nothing whatever about one's capabilities, and having her there didn't make me any better as a private eye, but image is everything in today's world, and you better not forget it.

Octavia was almost sixty—I suspected she might even be sixty, but didn't raise the question. Among the many things I've learned since being in business for myself is that older people are by far the better employees, particularly in a one-person office with no chance of meeting adorable guys or girl chums to gab with. Octavia is efficient, she likes to have the work and the money—I think the work is the more important— and I keep her happy by telling her enough about my cases to make her feel she's in my confidence. I suspect her of checking out the law in my cases. She's loyal to me, and I'm glad of that.

Before leaving the office, I'd asked Octavia to get me the catalog for the college I'd talked to Kate about, and particularly to get a course listing from the English department. She'd probably manage that before she came in tomorrow afternoon. Octavia can talk most people into giving her what she's after, which in her case is usually paper with information on it. I send her when I don't want to turn up in person just yet, or haven't the time. Yes, Octavia is permitted to offer bribes within reason, but we don't call them bribes; we call them recompense. It can be anything from a fancy lunch to cold cash.

I park my motorcycle in an alley down the street; I pay the super of the building to let me leave it there, which makes us both happy. I enjoy riding my motorcycle; most people with offices or homes on upper floors interviewing me, or I them, don't know how I got there. Mostly they don't notice my helmet, even if I'm unable to leave it with the receptionist, if any. New Yorkers aren't curious about each other outside of personal relationships, and that's one of the things I like best about New York. Riding a motorcycle is the only way to get around in the city without finding yourself stuck in traffic every other minute. I'm a champion of the subways, but they don't always go where I'm going. The main point is that I like how it feels to ride around on a motorbike; you see a lot more than from a car, and you can park between any two cars on the street in Midtown. Sometimes I get a ticket, but that's what I call the expense of doing business.

At home in Park Slope, I leave my bike in the areaway of the two-family house where I live; leaving it there was an arrangement I made when I rented the place, and it's worked out fine. The owner, with his second wife and assorted children, has the first floor, the basement, and the garden. I have the upper two floors—four rooms, not big, but I can move around when I feel like it, a kitchen, bath, and two fireplaces. I rarely make fires, but a fireplace is something I've always wanted and now have. There's no one to please but me. Nice.

I didn't go right home. I went to the health club near my office, which I do every day. I think the owner would happily pay me not to come, because I work out really hard and seem to suggest to his customers that this is not the way to lose weight. I don't take the hint, nor do I admit to the trainer there that I know I'm fat. All I'm interested in is being in good enough shape to deal with what happens, and he has to see I'm fit. Flabby private eyes don't last long, but it pays to look flabby; I know that.

What I might have told Kate Fansler, but don't mention to many people, is the advantage being fat gives me in my job, beyond looking vulnerable. You hear a lot of fancy tales about what private eyes do, and they're not untrue: sneaking into homes and offices, going through garbage, wearing a wire. All of that. But the real talent comes with getting people to talk, relax and talk. And that's where being fat helps. Whether it's because I seem unthreatening, because they can despise me for being fat, or because we like to think of fat people as comforting and nurturing, I'm not sure. Maybe it's because they don't have to bother to flirt with me. Whatever it is, I have great success in getting the gab going. Most people are dying to talk if you'll give them a chance. And the ones who play their cards close to the chest may not talk to anyone they perceive as a threat or a competitor, but with a nice fat lady of indeterminate age, hell, why not let it all hang out? I don't know the reason, but I would have liked to tell Kate Fansler that.

Once home, I took a shower, which I don't like to do at the gym; everybody walks around naked there, and it's not my scene. I wear sweats working out. Then I fixed dinner—takeout from the night before, reheated—poured some wine, and went on with my reading of a long, almost impenetrable article the victim, Charles Haycock, had recently written about Tennyson for a learned journal. I don't think I could have gotten through the damn thing without food and drink. All I'd managed to figure out by the time I'd finished eating was that the most important event in Tennyson's life happened before he was born, when his grandfather disinherited his father. I don't know if that's true, but it sure doesn't sound like a good reason to become a poet, even if Charles Haycock thought it did. Maybe Kate will explain it.

CHAPTER TWO

I am half sick of shadows.
—Tennyson, "The Lady of Shalott"

By the next afternoon, Octavia had the list of courses to be offered by the English department in the coming semester. Some years ago Clifton College had stopped offering course catalogs in all departments. Too expensive, Octavia had learned, and likely to be inaccurate by the time the actual semester rolled around. It was time to get the faculty straight in my mind, and the best way to do that was to win the confidence of (so I'd been told) the only person in any academic department who knows what is actually going on—as opposed to what is debated: the department's executive secretary. These women, and they are almost always women, have faculty status and are, together with their administrative colleagues, what keeps any academic institution from sudden collapse. The titular men above them in the hierarchy come and go and spend most of their time in committees, or raising funds, or in trying to get their agendas ratified by other men in power. The women do not run the college—more's the pity—but they keep it running. I'd learned that much from Claire Wiseman.

I spent the morning finishing up another inquiry, which had resolved itself faster than I had anticipated because the thief in question turned out to be a close relative of my client. Private settlement seemed indicated. Octavia and I made out a closing statement and sent it off.

That done, I contemplated the best way to approach the executive secretary of the English department and establish her confidence in me. I had a feeling she would answer questions; Octavia had chatted with her for a while and had told me something about Dawn Nashville. She was clearly a woman of integrity, a lonely woman whom most of the men in the office either took for granted or flirted with insincerely. She was divorced, and lived in New York City (like so many of those who work in New Jersey) with her mother, who, while neither ailing nor demanding, hardly offered the kind of attention Dawn might enjoy if it were ever offered to her.

I've often heard it said that nothing excites a lonely woman like an invitation. This is no doubt true of many women, but not as many as tradition would have it. That is, lonely women may like to be feted and made much of, but they would certainly, if they were as intelligent as Dawn Nashville, be suspicious of such sudden attentions.

I determined on a two-pronged strategy. First: I would ask her to have dinner with me at an elegant restaurant, not the highest on the list of those who want to be seen in the right places, but one that served good food and provided privacy with well-spaced tables. Second prong: I would be honest with her, explaining what I was after, if not altogether why, although she could gather that if she was as astute as she was reputed to be. It might take two dinners, but I thought my success depended on her liking and trusting me, above all on her finding my company enjoyable. I would not lie to her about anything, though I might defer an answer until later, in what someone told me was the manner of Sherlock Holmes with poor, obedient Watson.

The first dinner, which took place some days later, on a Friday night, which she preferred, was all I could have hoped for. I arranged it by telephone, but said I would pick her up and accompany her to the restaurant—in a taxi, not on my bike. I know that for women unaccustomed to going out at night, as I suspected she was, getting places was anxiety-inducing, if only moderately so. Also I didn't want to put her to any expense; I surmised that with her salary and her mother's social security and pension she was hardly awash in liquid assets.

She was waiting downstairs for me when my taxi pulled up. I had anticipated this—she was, after all, an efficient woman and a considerate one—and therefore did not ride my bike to her house, planning to reclaim it after I took her home, which would have been my natural procedure. I am a detective, and therefore intuitive, though I say so myself. Together we rode in my taxi to the restaurant, exchanging idle chatter until she could feel more comfortable. As I had hoped, she wanted to know how I became a private investigator. People always do, and in a situation like this, it's a good way to break the ice.

"Can anyone become a private investigator? I mean, do you have to have a degree of some sort?"

"Not as far as I know. You have to have worked for another investigator, or a company of investigators, for at least three years, and you have to pass an exam. For this you have to have irrefutable identification, and your fingerprints are taken. That's about it."

"Do you carry a gun?" she asked, as the taxi driver moved in and out of traffic lanes to little effect. That is often among the first questions asked me.

"I have a license to carry a gun. In New York State, it is not easy to get such a license, but properly accredited private investigators are allowed to have one."

"What about all those other people with guns—are they illegal?"

"Most of them are, particularly in the inner cities. But individuals can get a license for a gun for what is called target practice. Most of them live in rural areas, and are into a gun culture. All this, of course, applies only to concealed weapons, not to shotguns or rifles, which private eyes rarely mess with."

She smiled, and looked her question.

"No," I said, "I don't have it with me. I keep it locked up; I carry it only on dangerous assignments." I hoped the phrase didn't sound too phony in her ears, but like most honest citizens she found the life of a detective intriguing, and full of perilous encounters.

We reached the restaurant, and were greeted by the maître d' and seated with an adequate flourish. As it happened, I knew him, since I had had to watch one of his customers during a long evening, and occupy a table in the proper line of vision. I had of course paid handsomely for his help, and had since come a few times to dine there in a quite proper way. One thing you soon learn as a private investigator—though I didn't bother telling this to Dawn—is that the more people you can win to your side, usually through the expression of gratitude in the form of money, the better; they form a network of individuals essential to any detective.

I urged Dawn to order a cocktail, while I had vodka on the rocks. She said she didn't drink much, but would try a sherry. I doubted that this restaurant had sweet sherry, and didn't want to embarrass her into having to make a choice, so I ordered medium sherry for her. She sipped it slowly, whether from the desire to make it last or from distaste I couldn't tell, but she seemed happy.

"How did you get the name Dawn?" I asked. "It's a lovely name."

"Thank you," she said. It was clearly a compliment she was used to. "My parents waited a long time for a child; when I arrived they said that for them it was a new dawn."

"Isn't it great to be a welcome child?"

"They might have named me Benvenuta. One of the professors told me that. Benvenuto Cellini's father held him up when he was born and called out, 'Welcome.' In Italian, of course; that's what *benvenuto* means. I wasn't welcome once I had left home."

I wanted her compliant; I wanted all she could tell me, for sooner or later, and probably sooner, it would lead to the department where she had worked for ten years. I looked at her, waiting for more if she wanted to offer it then, but she didn't, and I didn't ask. It doesn't pay to waste the limited number of questions you can decently ask on an intrusive one that is also irrelevant. I urged her to have another glass of sherry, and she said she would if I had another drink too, so we did. Then we ordered. To my surprise—because she had been so diffident over the drink—she knew exactly what she wanted and requested it. I reminded myself that she was the highly efficient coordinator of a complicated department, and more interested in food than drink.

"How did you find an investigator to work for?" she asked me. "Did you know one?"

"I did. I used to be a public defender; there were a number of private investigators who worked with the lawyers, and one of them agreed to hire me."

"You were lucky." She looked into her glass, swirling the sherry around as though she thought it might yield an aroma. "Everything is contacts; I've learned that. But once you're a secretary, that's all people want you for. I get offered jobs as a secretary, but never as anything that would be a real step-up."

"Perhaps they would pay more?"

"They would. But working for the college, I get the same pension and health benefits as the faculty, and I can take two courses a year free. I've been taking one every semester, working toward my degree. These things are worth more than money."

"Very sensible," I said. "But I have heard that the academic world is not easy on its administrators, particularly those in departments. That may just be gossip or jealousy from those of us struggling in the big outside world." I had made my move; what she answered would determine the success of the evening. I've often had to return for another try after a conversation had dried up; it never pays to keep pushing immediately after you're blocked.

"I've thought of that," she said, polishing off her sherry with what I hoped was a sign of determination to spill her guts. I wasn't trapping her, after all. She wasn't the object of my queries; she was a means to an end, and I always try to reward my means somehow, if they come through, in this case by a good dinner. I smiled encouragingly as our food came.

She began on her appetizer. "Very good," she said. "You're right about the stresses. If you're at all a sympathetic person, someone who tries to be helpful, you get to hear from everyone about everyone else. Not that they have the least use for your opinion, not most of them, but they have to complain to someone who knows the cast of characters; at least, that's how I figure it. There's so much bad feeling."

"What is it that they get so worked up about?"

"Lots of minor things: they didn't get the classroom or the times they wanted. I do my best, but the final decision is made by the central administration. After all, they have more than one department to consider, and only a certain number of rooms and hours. But that's the least of it. They all differ on what should be taught and on which students should get fellowships and honors, on who should read whose senior thesis. That sort of thing. And then there's backbiting, nasty remarks, mean ones sometimes, particularly from the men about the women faculty. We hired one young woman, and I heard the men in the office—they seem to think I and the other women on the staff are deaf—call her a . . . well, a 'fuck bunny.' I walked out from my space and let them know I'd heard them; they didn't say that again. I remember when no one said a word like that, not in a college anyway."

I nodded my agreement, wondering what Dawn's experience in matters of crude sexual language had been. She was in her fifties; I'd looked up her statistics along with those of the rest of the faculty and staff—no big deal. Anyone who knows how to use a computer can do that. Earlier, one had to get access to a file cabinet; not much difference. She was a pretty woman, naturally so; her hair was dyed, but worn conservatively in what I call a bun but others call something fancier. Clearly efficient, she escaped, because of her age, the flirtatious attempts of many male professors. I'd learned also that the students had great affection for her—actually, Octavia had learned that. She's very good at gathering casual information for me; I may have to make her a partner one of these days, though my impression is that she prefers to pick up information on her own account, and offer it as a surprise, rather than being sent out officially to snoop. Getting printed information is, in Octavia's eyes, a matter requiring less talent and less challenging.

Dawn had ordered a steak and she seemed to be enjoying it. "I don't eat red meat very often, and it's a nice treat once in a while," she explained. She had a tendency to explain or apologize for everything, which I didn't try to stop: it's a habit that serves my purposes.

"Steak is no longer fashionable," I said, "but I think it's a great meal. It really gives you the sense that you've eaten something. As you might guess from looking at me, I like to eat."

"You have a very pretty face," she said. You'd be amazed how many people say that to me, and to almost all fat women, meaning: If you'd thin down you'd really be attractive. They never actually spell it out; implication is all.

"I sometimes think I started putting on weight in college because of my pretty face," I said. "I didn't really like guys coming after me all the time." This was quite untrue; I was a fat baby and never changed. But my aim in this conversation was to lead it where I wanted it to go; it worked.

"I know what you mean. Some of the male faculty are

really horrible. The girls look up to them, and they take advantage of it, or even encourage the shy ones. Not all the faculty, but most. I try to warn the girls sometimes, and some of them are grateful; others think I'm just jealous because I'm not their age. I guess most women have to learn about life for themselves."

I smiled and urged her to drink her wine; I'd ordered a bottle over her objections, pointing out that I like wine with my meal, and she might enjoy just sipping a little. I didn't want to talk about sex, not unless it led to some real anger; I wanted to talk about the real splits in the department. I said, "There's something I've always wanted to ask someone who could explain it to me; I don't meet many professors in my line of business." In fact, Kate Fansler, met only the other day, was my first professor to talk to, but I didn't bother adding that. I'd known Claire Wiseman, of course, but in an entirely different kind of case. "What do they fight about really? Do they think what they teach is more important than what the others teach, or is it a question of politics? We keep hearing about how the conservatives think the liberals have taken over the academic world. It's all very confusing to someone like me."

I looked at her hopefully, and poured a tiny amount of wine into her wineglass; I didn't want to overwhelm her or seem to be getting her drunk for nefarious purposes.

She took a sip. "I guess I've never really tasted good wine before," she said. "I always hate it; it tastes sort of sour, or else sweet."

I smiled gratefully. And waited.

"Professors are peculiar," she said. "The older ones have tenure, which means they can't ever be fired; you'd think that would make them secure, and they'd just go on doing whatever they got tenure for doing. But they still hate the thought that anyone might not want to hear what they have to say, or read what they write, or invite them to important conferences. The younger professors in the department, the ones without tenure, have different ideas sometimes, and it seems to me the older professors feel threatened. I don't know any of the details except in one case."

I smiled encouragingly and sipped my wine. It was good.

"There's a professor in the department, one of the most famous. He's an authority on Freud."

"Freud? I thought it was a literature department." I really was surprised to hear Freud mentioned, but I shouldn't have interrupted her. "Do go on," I urged.

"I don't attend the committees where the full professors decide on who to give tenure to, but news always leaks out. I know what happens because either they all talk about it in my office, or one of them tells me about it, to keep on my good side, or because they all like to talk and need to talk to someone who can follow what they're saying. Anyway, everyone in the department knows that if an assistant professor writes anything about Freud that questions anything about him, that's the end of that younger person's chance for tenure. He turned down a wonderful young woman because of that."

"But surely it takes more than one old professor to turn someone down?" I really wanted to understand this stuff.

"But there're always others who don't like the candidate. In this case she was a woman; she taught feminist texts, and suggested that Freud had been mistaken—or so I gathered. I don't really read all that the people in the department write; even if I could understand it, I haven't the time."

"It all sounds pretty petty to an outsider. Maybe all businesses are like that. But in most businesses, if you don't bring in the money, you don't get to keep the job. In a big detective firm, say, if you never solve any cases or satisfy any of the customers, you won't last long." I was determined to ask Kate what the point of tenure was, but it wasn't a question I really wanted Dawn's opinion on.

"It is petty," she said. "They're supposed to be dealing with great writing and eternal truths, and they act more like salesmen fighting over territory—that's what one of the other department secretaries said, and I thought it was true."

"Sure sounds it," I said. I decided not to question her any more; after a time, you begin to seem a little too interested in what they're saying, which is a good impression to avoid if you can.

Dawn went on: "The truth is, the department's changed a lot. We get very different students than when I began working there; of course, they're not all women anymore—Clifton used to be a women's college—but it's more than that. In those days, we got mostly well-off, anyway, middle-class kids, Americans, whose parents had been to college and sort of spoke the same language as the professors; I don't just mean English," she explained, quite unnecessarily, but I nodded understanding, "but how they look at the world and all. Today many come from other countries, and they're interested in peculiar things—well, some of them do seem peculiar to me, though I don't feel right in judging. 'Queer studies,' for instance, that's what they call it: the study of homosexuals in literature. And the study of imperialism and colonial peoples; and, of course, feminism. They also do a lot with race, and class, and that sort of thing. Many of the older professors want the students to concentrate on the classics—Chaucer, Shakespeare, Milton—and some students want to study more modern authors and the younger professors don't see why they shouldn't. It makes for a lot of trouble, I can tell you that, and the worst part is deciding who to hire and who to give tenure to. I try not to look back, but in the old days, there was a kind of good feeling in the department that just isn't there anymore."

"Sounds awful," I said, dismissing the subject. "Times change, and there's no doubt they're changing now. Shall we contemplate coffee and a really horrendous dessert?"

"Oh, I couldn't have coffee; I'd never get to sleep. I don't even dare to drink decaf."

"Dessert, then. I insist. This is your night to say boo to your diet."

The waiter came around with the dessert cart, and we each chose one. She had a hard time making up her mind, and I ordered the one she finally rejected so that I could offer her a bite, claiming a bite of hers, to be fair. She'd told me a lot, and I wanted her, in exchange, to have a good time. I suspected her life didn't include too many good times. I couldn't help wondering if any of those old professors ever took her out for a meal; somehow, I doubted it. Later, I dropped Dawn at her home, and took the taxi on to Park Slope. I've never understood how people can keep cars in Park Slope; there's never anywhere to put them. A guy I know calls it Double-Park Slope. Thank the lord for my landlords, their area space, and my bike.

* * *

My next obvious task was to interview some of the professors myself, to try to narrow my list of professors down to those who might be suspects in Charles Haycock's murder. Dawn had given me a sense of the atmosphere in the whole department; it hardly encouraged me to think that was enough to make my interviews productive. The professors might agree to see me once in a murder investigation of one of their number, but a repeat might not be so easy to arrange. I had to make the first interview count, at least until my suspicions were a little more directed.

It seemed only natural to consult Kate Fansler at this point. She would certainly have some suggestions, and—this was a thought I was a bit ashamed of, but upon which I was, all the same, determined—I wanted to see if her husband, Reed Amhearst, who had connections in the D.A.'s office, could get me in touch with the police detective on the case, even though the case was in New Jersey, where Clifton College was. Police officers do offer their colleagues from other places a certain amount of courtesy. I was sure that if the police who were handling the case and I could combine information we could both do better, but it's far from easy to convince the police of this. They don't like private eyes messing around in their cases. It would have to be a special favor, and maybe Reed Amhearst could manage it.

I took a shower and, back in my sweats, sat down

with a pad and pen to plan out my questions for Kate Fansler. Sure, I knew I could have waited to see her; probably I *should* have waited to see her. But I really did need to get my head cleared about English departments; families are much more common ground to me. People say that all families are different, but for my money they're all pretty much the same. My hope was that all academic departments were pretty much the same too, so I could really get a handle on this from my own investigations and with Kate Fansler's help.

Besides, I wouldn't mind seeing Banny again.

CHAPTER THREE

The real Oxford is a close corporation of jolly, un-tidy, lazy, good-for-nothing, humorous old men who have been electing their own successors ever since the world began and who intend to go on with it.

—C. S. Lewis, in a letter to his brother

When I called Kate Fansler for another appointment, I offered to go to her office. This seemed more professional and fairer to her than intruding upon the privacy of her home. But, having thanked me for my consideration, she told me to come to her house as before. "You'll want to see Banny again," she said, "and I can hardly take her to the university. Dogs are forbidden on the campus, and she's so big that people with dog phobias become hysterical and have to be carted off to the infirmary."

I agreed, thanking her. My own interpretation, not to undermine her generosity and hospitality, was that she hardly wanted to be seen consulting a private investigator about a fairly famous academic murder at another college. Kate was by now, I supposed, fairly well known as a detective, and the murder at Clifton College was the topic of the moment; I thought her keeping her work as a snoop away from her colleagues was a good idea.

Not that I wasn't grateful to be going to her apartment, seeing Banny and seeing her in her own space, so to speak; I was damn glad of the chance. But one figures things out for oneself; one has to, no distrust intended.

Banny recognized me, which was a nice compliment. She actually got up, huge tail wagging, and walked over to me after Kate had opened the door. I dropped my helmet in the outside hall, gave Banny a really good doggy greeting and Kate a modified one, and followed both hosts into the living room. Once seated, I denied being thirsty, and pulled out my notes. I figured I owed it to Kate to get right down to business.

But Kate had noticed me dropping my helmet outside her door, as she had not last time. Somehow, the fact that I ride a motorbike fascinates even the most sophisticated people; they want to know why, and how, and if I ever give someone else a ride.

"No, I don't. For one thing, they haven't a helmet. For another, while there's theoretically room behind me, there *isn't* much room behind me. How come you noticed my helmet this time? You didn't notice it on my first visit."

"Reed noticed it when he came in the last time you were here. He said, 'I see she rides a motorbike,' and I asked how he knew, since I'm supposed to be the detective in the family, and he mentioned the helmet, gallantly admitting that had he been inside when you arrived, rather than arriving from outside, he wouldn't have noticed it either."

I nodded and returned to my notes. But she was still in a questioning mood.

"Why do you always mention being . . . well, heavy?" she asked. "I know that's not a very tactful question, but if I don't come right out with it, I'll be thinking of it through all our conversations, which would, you admit, be distracting. So forgive me and answer."

"Would you start out asking a black woman why she referred so often to her race?"

I could see I had embarrassed her.

"Kate, please. Being fat's my hang-up, the cross I bear rather less gladly than I might; that's a quotation from a hymn, in case they didn't make you go to church. All the other nasty jokes are now forbidden, but not against fat people. Example: someone gave me a collection of short stories, detective stories, by women, and here's how one by Sue Grafton begins. I've been lugging the book around with me to read while waiting for appointments, so I happen to have it here, as evidence. Grafton is describing a woman waiting outside her office. 'She was short and quite plump, wearing jeans in a size I've never seen on the rack. Her blouse was tunic-length, ostensibly to disguise her considerable rear end.' Later, Grafton's detective goes to see a relative of this woman and notes that, like the first one, 'she was decked out in a pair of jeans, with an oversize T-shirt hanging almost to her knees. It was clear big butts ran in the family.'* See what I mean?"

Kate seemed to be searching for something to say. I kept on talking, to give her a moment. I guess I really wanted her to understand how I felt about this fat stuff.

"Look," I said, "being fat's been a lot of use to me. You can believe that. It's gotten me confidences I'd never have had otherwise. But I don't see why thin has to be a qualification for looking down on others, the way white used to be. I've made it a kind of crusade. But I do agree, it can get boring as a subject, and I'll try not to mention it again. Now, can I tell you—"

"It isn't boring, and I'm perfectly willing and happy to have you talk about it, now that you know I've mentioned it so we both don't have to pretend you're not saying what you're saying. I do hope you see what I mean."

"I do, and I'm grateful you brought it out in the open. If there's one thing I hate more than another, it's tact. Not real tact, maybe, but the kind where you

---

* Sue Grafton, "A Poison That Leaves No Trace," in *Sisters in Crime 2* (New York: Berkley, 1990), pp. 90, 97.

know they're being tactful. I meet up with a lot of that. It doesn't deserve the name 'tact,' does it?"

"I'm pretty tired of tact," Kate said. "It's mostly a technique useful to those trying to get away with something." She looked at her watch. "I'd like a drink. Can I offer you something? I'm having Scotch, but you can have whatever you want. It is well after five."

" 'And as the sun sinks my thirst rises.' I had an uncle who used to say that. If you don't mind, I'll wait till I've gotten through these notes and heard what you have to say. I've got to go and see these professors, and it's absolutely new terrain for me. Maybe after I've talked to you, I won't sound quite so ditsy. It's not exactly in my usual line of work."

"Perhaps you'll make a specialty of it when this case is over," Kate said. She went across the room, where there was liquor and ice and everything, and made herself a drink. I agreed to have a glass of seltzer, and settled down. I hoped Scotch didn't affect her too much, but what the hell. At least she made me feel welcome. Banny's eyes followed Kate's passage across the room, but Banny didn't move; Kate wasn't going anywhere.

Kate sipped her drink. "Claire Wiseman told me that the department sounded like a business the owners were trying to wrest from one another. She seems to know someone who used to work there, and her tales are pretty harrowing, Claire says. Not that I've ever been an admirer of small colleges in the countryside; there's far too much togetherness and far too much interest in one another's lives. In a university in New York City, like mine, we all go home at night and fade into a different, largely private world. Certainly there are departmental struggles, but they aren't each professor's whole life. Also, small departments are either pleasant or hell. Tell me about this one—the details, I mean. I know you can't make any judgments yet." She took another sip and sat back, all attention.

I took a deep breath and peered at my notes, though I had them by heart. It does no good to sound too knowledgeable before those who may offer information; it's best if they feel themselves to be the authority in the matter, which of course they usually are, to some extent. I didn't act differently with Kate.

"It's a department of ten professors," I reported, "six tenured, four not. Divided, as I suppose all English departments are, into periods, or maybe they should be called fields, or areas—I'm not too clear on that. Anyway, the periods or fields, in no particular order, are Victorian—well, there is a particular order here, because that was Haycock's field, and he's the reason we're talking about all this. I know you said most professors aren't given to murder, but are English departments more given to murder than most?"

"Not as far as I know," Kate said. "The only act

comparable to murder I know of personally was a suicide. A new assistant professor was found to have plagiarized his dissertation and his book; he killed himself before the matter went far, thus proclaiming his guilt, or so everyone thought. That's about it. Do go on."

"Well, in addition to Victorian, we have American, Modern—I'm not sure what that is, exactly—Medieval, Renaissance, Romantics/Seventeenth Century, Eighteenth Century, and something Comparative. Most of these have a full professor attached to them, lord of all he surveys, so to speak."

"That's a new and insightful way to put it," Kate said. "Go on."

"The leftover fields are covered by assistant professors. Sometimes one of these chaps, or an assistant professor, teaches the novel. There's also a part-time person who teaches creative writing, which, I gathered, is there to bring in the money from people in the neighborhood who are yearning to become published writers." (It was Octavia who gathered this, but I saw no point in saying so.) "The person teaching it last year and this year is named Kevin Oakwood, a writer I've never heard of. And that's about it. The only one of these fields with a woman running it—that's probably not the right term—is Modern. I think that may be a part of the trouble with Haycock—he hated professional women, or so it seems. And two of the three assistant professors are women. I did learn that there's a lot of turnover in the junior faculty; two on tenure-track lines—I hope I'm impressing you with my newfound lingo—were new last year and stick together. It was over the promotion of one of the assistant professors who'd actually stuck around a while that the war of the sexes broke out in the rolling fields of New Jersey."

"Professor Haycock took his cue from Tennyson when it came to women," Kate said. "Hold on a minute while I get a book. It's a quote too suitable to Haycock to miss." Kate left the room, then came back, turning the pages of a book—the poems of Tennyson, I was detective enough to deduce.

"Here we are: 'Woman is the lesser man, and all thy passions matched with mine / Are as moonlight unto sunlight, and as water unto wine.' That's from 'Locksley Hall.' And, to do Tennyson and Haycock full justice, we ought to add another couple of lines from 'Locksley Hall': 'He will hold thee, when his passion / Shall have spent its novel force / Something better than his dog, a little dearer than his horse.' "

"Was Tennyson serious?" I asked.

"Ah, you'll have to ask a Tennyson expert that. But I'll try to brush up on that exalted poet. I used to quite like him, but I never admitted it; he wasn't the accepted cup of tea when I was young, and probably isn't now. But he could write neat lines."

Kate paused, as if reminded of something. "But you know, he did write one famous line that still bothers me after all this time; it's one of his prize bits: 'Now lies the earth all Danaë to the stars,' from a lyric called 'Now sleeps the crimson petal.' An immortal line, beautiful. But what disturbs me is that Zeus came to Danaë, whose father had locked her up to prevent her getting pregnant, in a shower of gold. The Greek gods always found a way to screw the women they were after. But the stars do not affect the earth in any way; the earth does not lie vulnerable to the stars. So it's a weak, fanciful metaphor, though a gorgeous one, describing a clear night in the country."

There was a pause as I took this in. "You know, Kate," I finally said, allowing an edge to creep into my voice, "there is no doubt that you're going to be a big help to me in this case."

"I'm glad you appreciate that." Kate grinned. "Leave me the lists of courses and faculty, the whole thing, and I'll be ready to talk about it in a more coherent way then, when I've got the whole department and faculty straight."

"So I guess I should be going now," I said. I, who usually couldn't wait to be on my way, seemed to be lingering. I gathered up my notes and the book I'd been reading from.

But Kate held up a hand. "You have to realize that you're likely to do better than I would in this particular investigation. I'd be handling too much baggage to be able to see the situation with any clarity. I've been an academic for too long. I'm unlikely to view things in a new light. I'd have expectations and knowledge of how an English department works on the inside."

"That sounds like an advantage to me. I've learned as an investigator that you can't know too much about a situation; you rarely know enough."

"True. But I think in this case, with murder a possibility, a fresh look and new impressions might be worth a lot—and you can always get the fruits of my long experience here when you feel need of them. Your perceptions of these people and what they're like—that's what you ought to be going along with, for a while at least." She seemed to reflect on her words.

"Nonetheless," she went on, "there is some information that might be worth having before you talk to the personnel and gain impressions of the scene. That is, the background of the academic situation you'll be observing and how it came about—in a very general sort of way, of course. When my generation of professors was getting tenure, the academic picture was a lot rosier than it is today. Never mind the reasons for the change—there's some disagreement about that—but no one debates the effect: there is too little money for faculty, too few positions for the generation of new Ph.D.'s coming along. There's a general exploitation of new Ph.D.'s, hiring them part-time and as adjuncts, where they make too little money with no benefits and no real part to play in the department."

"Why do the departments keep turning out Ph.D.'s if there are no jobs?" I asked. "Or is that one of those questions for which there is an obvious answer I'm not bright enough to see?"

"On the contrary. I'm telling you all this because the real answer is not widely admitted. Why do the major universities, and even the second-rank universities, continue to turn out Ph.D.'s? The university wants the money, they want the population so that they can keep their place in the world, and the professors prefer teaching graduate students, who are self-selected for literary studies and smart, to teaching college-age kids whose desire to learn is hardly passionate; they're inspired by quite different passions in those years. But above all, the senior professors want graduate students to teach the introductory courses, like literature surveys and composition, so that they don't have to teach them themselves. As it happens, the graduate students make very good teachers; they're enthusiastic, new to teaching experience, excited to be in the life they've always dreamed about. But that's hardly permanent; once they've done their stint, they're on their own with no jobs in sight, or very few."

"Don't professors like teaching?" I asked. "Isn't that why they're professors?"

"Possibly that's why they wanted to be professors. Some of them are great teachers, but that isn't how you get ahead in the academic world—not even in a small college like Clifton. You're supposed to publish. No one will read what you've published. No one is really interested most of the time—but if you haven't published you're not a respected academic. So what every professor wants is time to research and write a book— any book. For an assistant professor today to be promoted to associate professor, they are often expected to have published more than any of the established professors of my generation or older have published in their whole lives."

"This is a joke, right?"

"No joke. Also, teaching gets tiresome. The students have read less and less, often can't write worth a damn, even in graduate school—I'd hate to tell you how many dangling modifiers I've corrected in my time! And the time off professors get—sabbaticals and summers—are the highly sought rewards of the profession."

I nodded, trying not to let my expression reveal that

I didn't know what a dangling modifier was. It sounded vaguely improper.

"Teaching's not what it is about," Kate continued, speaking I thought more to herself than me. "Not after the first few years, anyway. And those for whom teaching is a joy, those who don't long for time off, don't get tenure; they certainly don't get the thanks of their academic institution. They used to; not anymore."

"But people keep on getting Ph.D.'s in English."

"Right. And they hate their professors, among other reasons you may unearth, because there are no jobs; certainly few good jobs. And the older guys, the established ones, don't like being resented. There's a lot more than that—arguments over fields, subject matter, new genres of criticism—but I'm leaving you to find that out on your own. A college like Clifton may be very different from a university of the sort I'm used to."

"It sounds as though murder is not as unlikely as I thought."

"There's a great deal of anger and fear. Whether or not that leads to murder is a question; I doubt it, but I used to doubt a lot of things that have recently become quite ordinary."

I sighed. She was right. I didn't want to be burdened with more than the general picture; I wanted to decide about the characters in this story without having to fight against Kate's impressions, with which I would probably be tempted to agree.

"Well," I said, a bit too plaintively, "at least I can ask you about Tennyson, can't I?"

"By all means; I'm always ready to bone up on poetry and literary criticism, particularly of figures I haven't ever taught or even thought about in years. But Tennyson may not turn out to be the motive here."

"He very well may be. Anyway, that's what Claire Wiseman thought; that's mainly why I was supposed to consult you." I sighed, and started to my feet again. Tomorrow I'd begin interviewing these folks.

"I forgot to tell you," Kate said. "That's me—babbling on about the academic world and forgetting practicalities. Reed has found you a detective sergeant in the New Jersey police who's ready to pass the time of day. He owes Reed one, is how Reed put it."

"I don't like to think of Reed calling in his chips on my account."

"Don't worry. I suspect Reed suspects, or anyway hopes, that you're the only reason he will ever have to call in a chip from New Jersey. I'd offer you a drink now, but it occurs to me that drinking and driving don't go together any better on a motorcycle than in an automobile."

"True, alas."

"You'll have to come one evening on public transportation," Kate said. "We'll have a lovely tipple when this is over, or even underway."

"Right," I said. Banny, to my delight, got up to see me out. I suspected this was less affection than the thought of some treat that would materialize when I was out of the way. But all acts of affection are welcome, I thought, worrying about tomorrow, and wondering how soon I'd have an excuse to see Kate again.

CHAPTER FOUR

How fares it with the happy dead?
—Tennyson, *In Memoriam*

I had planned to visit Clifton College the next day, but when I returned home from my visit to Kate, there was a message from Donald Jackson, calling, he said, at the suggestion of Reed Amhearst. This was Reed's New Jersey policeman whom Kate had mentioned. So I arranged to meet with him before facing the Clifton English department. I could, of course, have interviewed most of the faculty in New York, where, like Dawn, many of them lived; few, it seemed, were prepared to live in New Jersey.

I have never understood what this odd prejudice is against New Jersey. Certainly the view from their side of the Hudson—a view of Manhattan—beats any vista New York itself can provide. But emerging on my bike from the Lincoln Tunnel, I had to admit that the scenery along the Jersey Turnpike certainly suggested nothing pleasant or inviting. Still, I supposed, one suburb was very like another, and none of them my choice of a place to live. The only real differences I had ever found between one suburb and another was the distance between the houses, and the size of the lawns.

Donald Jackson told me to meet him in a bar not too far from the college. He had explained, when I returned his call, that he didn't want to meet in the police station, and that he thought we ought to talk before I took on the English department or any part of the college. A good idea, I thought.

I found the bar and the detective without any trouble; he was in a booth, and I could see why he had chosen the place. It was a local sort of bar not suited either to the students or the nearby suburban folk. The police didn't meet each other socially in this town, and weren't likely to stick their heads in here; Donald Jackson and I were quite unnoticed. In fact, it was my kind of place—working class, with big sandwiches and breakfast all day. We each ordered coffee; he had a hamburger and I had breakfast, my favorite meal: bacon, eggs, home fries, and toast.

He told me he was called Don, and I told him I was called Woody. He was tall, muscular, handsome—a black man who knew just how attractive he was to women; I for one would never again wonder why they kept starring Denzel Washington in every second movie. I worried that the first sight of me would disappoint him; I always worry about that. I didn't ask why he owed Reed, and he didn't tell me. He treated me just right, like he was ready for now to respect a new colleague, giving me the benefit of the doubt. I thought we could probably work together just fine.

"If I've got this straight," he said, "you're a private eye hired by the college to find out who offed their Professor Haycock."

"That's about it," I said, "except that the family hired me before anyone in the English department did. I've sort of spread out my investigation to the college since that anonymous letter. A member of the family may have done it, but somehow I don't see it. That doesn't mean I may not see it any day soon."

"That's how I figured it. We were originally called in by the family too, and now we're supposed to be looking at everybody, including the college. But between you and me, I don't think that the police are going to get very far here. The idea seems to be that the main suspect is a woman who didn't show the proper respect for some poet who's been dead a century, give or take a year."

"Yes," I said. The bacon and eggs were great, but I tried to keep my mind on the conversation. He asked if he could try my potatoes and I said he sure could. I thought that was the most tactful request I'd heard from man or woman in years, maybe ever. I saved it up for Kate, to show her an example of real tact: making someone who was female, fat, a private eye, and not usually welcomed by the police, feel good. Real tact.

"The poet Tennyson." I groaned. "Fortunately I'm getting some help on the literary side of things, but colleges are not exactly my usual place of operation either." I didn't mention that it was Reed's wife who was assisting me. Don probably knew it, but he'd respect me for not spilling everything—just the stuff he needed to know, and from him, the stuff I needed to know. Which was plenty.

"I haven't seen so much infighting since we had to look into some guys who were shaving points in a basketball play-off," he said. "There's a lot of money involved there. But, hey, I like one country singer, I'm not going to blow you away because you like a different one who may dislike mine, if you follow me."

"You might if your reputation, which in the academic world is the same as money, or just about, were tied up in one singer or another. I mean, if I've written five books on a poet, and you think he's not only dead but gone for all practical purposes, and if you tell the students that, and furthermore, if you try to promote a young scholar who agrees with you . . ."

"I get it," he said, obviously afraid I'd never manage

to finish the sentence. "But do you drop little heart pills, digoxin, into his drink because he doesn't like what you have to say about his poet?"

"We may never get it," I said. "But . . ."

"It would help you if I filled you in on where we are in our investigation, which isn't far, but we've at least eliminated a few of the suspects, that is to say, in the faculty."

I took out my notebook. "I appreciate this," I said. "I've talked to the department secretary, but I'm not what you'd call clued in."

"You'd need an advanced degree for that," he said. "Here's how it looks: There are about twelve of them on the faculty, counting two part-timers. One of them teaches writing and the other is filling in for two courses for the professor on leave. At least we can eliminate two of the faculty, both men. One is on his 'sabbatical' "—Don put the word in sneering quotation marks—"and one is on 'paternal leave.' " The second sneer I rather expected was not forthcoming. "I wish I'd had paternal leave when my kids were born," he said to my surprise.

Great, I thought. I'm going to grab this guy and take him home for my very own. I wish. "That leaves ten," I said. "Enough to get straight. Isn't one of the ten Haycock?"

"Sure enough, smart lady. But maybe he killed himself and tried to blame it on the woman who didn't think much of his country singer; we've got to count him in."

"Okay by me, but can't we eliminate any of the others on the grounds that they weren't at Haycock's house the day he died? I know that isn't supposed to have eliminated the wife, but the faculty?"

"They were all there. Start-of-term party, always given by one of the senior guys. Except: Not only was the wife absent, so was the chief suspect—if one believes the anonymous letter, the only senior woman in the department."

"The one who made nasty about Haycock's poet."

"The very one. And that lady professor was there, if only for a few minutes, but after the bottle was uncorked. She dropped in to say she was sorry about not coming to the party, some important previous engagement, but she offered some dish she'd made for the party. Anyway, as far as I can see, Haycock was asking for it. He always drank retsina. Ever tasted it?"

I shook my head.

"It's Greek," Don went on. "Haycock developed a liking for it when he visited Greece. Probably his poet was Greek or something. Anyway, it's made from resin and it tastes like detergent; I tried it. You could put just about anything in it, sure it wouldn't be noticed. No doubt he thought it clever to be known as the drinker of such awful stuff.

"I knew the pills were in the retsina. But that didn't mean pills could have been dropped in the wine bottle at any time. It was only opened that afternoon by Haycock himself, before the party. So the person who put in the digoxin pills had to have been there. Remember, the great thing about putting the pills in retsina is that nobody else was likely to drink it. It's a wonder anyone ever did."

"Right," I said. "But from what I've learned, digoxin is so potent that only tiny doses of it are needed, and it works so fast it might not have mattered if the victim tasted it or not. Maybe the murderer didn't know that and decided to play it safe. I still don't see how the wife could have done it; she was definitely not there."

"I never thought much of the wife as a suspect," Don said, "though I suppose she could have doctored the drink and somehow gotten the cork back in and the bottle all sealed up, which is a bit far-fetched." He reached for money to pay the bill, gesturing to cut my protests off. "Next meal's on you," he said. We got up from the booth as he went on talking. "It didn't seem to me she had a motive worth anything, in spite of the son's suspicions; she lacked opportunity; and the only circumstantial evidence against her is that she knew he took those pills. I know, I know, poisoning is supposed to be a woman's crime, but you certainly couldn't prove it by me."

Outside, I pointed to my bike. "Yeah," he said, "Reed told me about that. I brought my helmet." He must have left it near the door; now he waved it at me.

I stood there stunned, looking idiotic, which was how I felt.

"Do you mind dropping me off near the station house? I like riding on motorbikes." I was so obviously unhappy, he patted me on the shoulder.

"Don't tell me you don't have a license or something." I shook my head. "What's the problem? Did you just learn to drive this thing?" He was really puzzled, and I could see that for the first time I was worrying him.

"I'm not sure you'll fit on the back," I said. "It's a small seat, and I'm pretty large." It was the truth, and the only excuse for my hesitation, but I hated to have to say it.

"Shit," he said. "I've ridden on smaller seats in back of bigger people. Let's go. And if I fall off because there wasn't enough room, I promise not to sue you."

Gritting my teeth, I put on my helmet and got on the bike. He slid up easily behind me and, as soon as I had it started, put his arms around my waist. "Just keep straight on," he shouted in my ear. "I'll tap you when we hang a left."

There was nothing to it, really—nothing. I wished I didn't like his arms around me, I wished I wasn't so fat where he was holding me, but mostly I enjoyed it. He got off near the station—not wanting to be asked about his lift, I suspected—and told me he'd be in touch. I told him where I was staying, and he said, "You know my numbers," and was gone.

I followed his directions to the college, feeling as if I'd just been given a gift. Wake up, Woody, I told myself. Wake the fuck up! He's a policeman, and he's probably got a neat agenda of his own. All right, he's doing Reed a favor, but don't let him get you on his side without a struggle. You may not end up agreeing about who done it. Remember that, Woody, I said to myself. But I felt a small glow, like the glow I'd felt with Kate, only a bit more electric. You watch out, I told myself, or you'll start acting like all those fool women you have to track down or whose husbands you have to track down. Shape up, I told myself.

To sober up, I made myself think about digoxin, the oldest and most widely known way to bump someone off quickly. It's the poison of choice in many books with murder plots, because it's so easy to get hold of, relatively speaking. The book of poisons I had looked up foxglove flowers in said as the source of digitalis, it was the oldest cardiac medicine, used hundreds of years ago to treat something they called dropsy and we call congestive heart failure. It's readily available, even as a pill, but if push comes to shove you can buy foxgloves at a florist and extract the stuff yourself. Haycock had been given enough to kill ten people, maybe twenty. Now that was a sobering thought.

But it was the sight of the college that really sobered me. It looked like the set for one of those movies they used to make in the Forties. My mother always loved them, and dragged me along with her to revival houses to see them. I expected June Allyson to come chirping out onto the quadrangle at any moment. But what approached as I stopped to ask where the English department hung out was a man who did recognize me as a woman in my helmet and who didn't think motorbikes belonged on his precious campus. My being a woman made him a little less nasty about it. Or maybe he thought a big dame on a motorbike was not going to take bullying too easily.

I lifted the helmet and smiled. "I'll leave it in the parking lot," I said. "Then, how do I find my way to the English department? I'm expected, and they won't be too happy to be told I was stopped by campus security." Total bullshit, but how was he to know? If you're thin, you bat your eyelashes. If you're fat, you throw your weight around. It almost always works.

"The English department's in that building," he said, pointing to something in the near distance covered in ivy. "And walk your bike to the parking lot back there. Motorbikes aren't what they want around here."

I obeyed meekly. Knowing when meekness gets you what you want is a P.I.'s best tool, and much easier to do if you're female. He nodded, watching me push the bike toward the parking lot. I was thinking he was a lot easier to handle than the professors in the English department were going to be.

Once I'd parked the bike, reached the right building on foot, and climbed the stairs to the English department—I avoid elevators; they can get stuck or, worse, force you into close contact with someone you don't want to meet—I greeted Dawn and asked which professor I might talk to now. She gave me a list of the faculty, and helped me to match the names up with the fields. I'd brought a list of those with me. Haycock I knew was Victorian, or had been, and I knew the only woman full professor was Modern. Her name turned out to be Antonia Lansbury.

"Any relation to Angela?" I asked. Talk about women detectives on television; that Lansbury dame played a woman who never went anywhere without tripping over a body, but I liked the actress: not young, and not into romance.

"A distant cousin, I think," Dawn said. "Antonia's

teaching, but she'll probably be here later, if you want to wait for her. She always sees students in her office after her classes, which is more than the men do. Anyway, most of them. You could find her then."

"I might," I said. Now I wanted to get the names of the others. American was a guy named Donald Goldberg; he just got tenure, Dawn advised me in a whisper— terrible fight, the department was divided, but the dean and the president got him in.

"Do things often work out that way?" I asked, also in a whisper.

"Mostly the dean and the president turn people down," she hissed back. "This caused a lot of comment, I can tell you."

"I hope you will, one day, when you let me buy you another dinner. I did enjoy that one so much."

"I did too," Dawn said. I had the impression not a lot of people took the time to be nice to Dawn. Lucky for me, though that didn't make me glad.

We returned to the list. Medieval turned out to be a very nice guy named Larry Petrillo; that is, Dawn thought him nice, and said the students did too. I figured out he was probably not as big a pompous ass as the others. Renaissance—which means mainly Shakespeare, according to Dawn—was named David Longworth, an older man, close to retirement if he ever decided to retire, which nobody had to these days, not the way it used to be: sixty-five and you were out. You couldn't celebrate your sixty-sixth birthday standing up in a classroom. Then, also probably long in the tooth, was the Freud fanatic Dawn had told me about; his name was Daniel Wanamaker, and his field was more or less Nineteenth Century, and Comparative, meaning Germany and France. Those were the full professors. The assistant professors were David Lermann, Eighteenth Century, and Eileen Janeer, Romantic; she also covered Seventeenth Century this year, since the third assistant professor was away on a fellowship; she had been in England the whole time, visiting holy places where seventeenth-century divines sermonized. Well, as my mom used to say, it takes all sorts.

I made a list of the professors and held it out to Dawn for verification. She nodded affirmation. The list read:

VICTORIAN—CHARLES HAYCOCK
 (DECEASED)
AMERICAN—DONALD GOLDBERG
MODERN—ANTONIA LANSBURY
MEDIEVAL—LARRY PETRILLO
RENAISSANCE—DAVID LONGWORTH
COMPARATIVE—DANIEL WANAMAKER

ROMANTIC—EILEEN JANEER, ASSISTANT
   PROF.
EIGHTEENTH CENTURY—DAVID
   LERMANN, ASSISTANT PROF.
NOVEL—JANET GRAHAM
WRITING—KEVIN OAKWOOD
(ONE ASSISTANT PROF. ON LEAVE)

"So who's around?" I asked. I thought I might as well get started; after all, I had to begin sometime.

"At this hour, most of them are teaching," Dawn said. "But David Longworth's in his office." She pointed me in the right direction.

I knocked on the door of Professor Longworth's office, even though it was open. I didn't like to barge right in. He looked up and waved me in. I had the feeling he would have been glad to see anyone. He looked kind of expectant, sitting there, and I felt sorry for him.

"Come in, come in," he shouted, waving even more vigorously. I walked up to his desk and introduced myself.

"I'm a private investigator," I said. I always pause there for some expression of amazement, curiosity, or dismay.

"Surely you have a name," he said. "Even Shakespeare's fools had names, most of them."

"Woodhaven," I said. "People call me Woody Woodhaven."

"Nicely alliterative," he said. "Sit down. I suppose you're the one they hired to find out who rushed Chuck Haycock into shuffling off his mortal coil. *Hamlet,*" he added as I looked a trifle puzzled.

"Yes, that's me." Or is it *I*? I wondered. Talking with professors always makes me nervous. On the one hand, I think most of them haven't the wit to come in out of the rain; on the other hand, they make me feel stupid. Not a good combination, if you want the truth.

Professor Longworth didn't seem bothered by my grammar, right or wrong. These days he was probably used to anything; no doubt he considered himself lucky if anyone read Shakespeare, let alone talked like him.

"Ask away," he said. "You will want to know where I was on the afternoon Chuck met his Maker. Well, I was with Chuck, as was everyone else in the department, so you'd better consider me a prime suspect." He seemed pleased with the idea.

"At the moment I'm trying to get a picture of the department, how it works, and how the professors relate to each other, that kind of thing. I came to you first because you've been here the longest and probably have the most measured view." This was also a crock, but flattery always works.

"That's very sensible of you," he said. "Most people think the longer one has been here, the less one knows. We older faculty may not be as familiar with rock stars as we ought, but we've seen all the cycles come and go, and we have some sense of what works and what doesn't. Not that anyone wants to hear it. Or anything else, for that matter. Can you imagine teaching *Lear* to a classroom of sophomores these days?"

"They must be interested if they take it."

"It's required," he said. "I'd be a very lonely man otherwise. Lear complained about ungrateful children; he should have met today's undergraduates. But you didn't come to hear the woes of teaching Shakespeare."

"It all helps to get the picture. Surely they listen to you in faculty meetings," I said. I doubted it, but I had to get him off Shakespeare and onto more practical subjects. I plan to read all of Shakespeare when I retire, but he's not on the top of my list at the moment.

"My dear young woman, if you suppose that, you can't be a very good detective. Surely you have already concluded that nobody listens to me. Not unless they want something; what do you want to know?"

"Tell me about faculty meetings," I said, not looking embarrassed. I was even getting to like the old chap.

"Ah. Now you're sounding like a detective. Faculty meetings are where we all get off our high horses and sound like boys in a frat house deciding on whom to pledge."

"Really?" I said. Old Longworth was beginning to surprise me.

"As near as makes no matter, I do assure you."

"You do have a tenured woman on the faculty; hasn't she made any difference?"

"Apart from the other professors wishing they could frankly admire her legs, no."

I think my mouth dropped open at this. I shut it, but couldn't decide if he was trying to tell me the woman had good legs, or they wished she had. He sensed my question.

"She has great legs, but she doesn't think that's the part of her accoutrement they ought to be considering, and she's quite right. I'm afraid most of the men in this department haven't greeted women's lib with open arms. Tony—Antonia—has to sit in on any interview with a female candidate to keep the old boys from admiring *her* legs."

"Was Professor Haycock like that?" I asked.

"Leader of the pack. His hatred of women scholars, and Tony in particular, was the one fact everyone in the department agreed upon."

"Do you dislike her?"

"I don't. She's nice to me, which is sufficiently

unusual around here to win my affection. Beyond that, I admire her. She could have settled in as one of the boys, and written a book showing how women had ruined the wonders men had contrived, but she didn't. She's not a queen bee—I bet you didn't think I knew that term— and she really fought to get another tenured woman into the department. That really fluttered the dove- cotes; imagine, two women sitting in on meetings of the tenured faculty."

He looked positively gleeful at the memory. Since Professor Longworth seemed ready enough to gossip about his colleagues, I didn't want to lose the moment. He might tell me things he wouldn't tell me at another time, starting from scratch. When interviewees talk, keep them talking—that's my motto.

"Surely all the professors don't think exactly alike?" I said, astonishment ringing in my voice.

"Each had his separate reason for turning down Catherine Dorman for tenure."

"Such as?" I asked encouragingly.

"Haycock I've already mentioned. He was the only one who admitted he was against women, period. The others were sophisticated enough not to put it quite so plainly, to say nothing of affirmative action rules. They didn't like her last ten refereed articles, or she was not properly obsequious to Freud—that was the opinion of our chairman, Daniel Wanamaker, who, as I understand it, is seriously considering retiring and taking his ante-diluvian opinions to the South."

"And who will be chairman when he does leave?"

"A good question, my dear. Who indeed? I would like the job, and I'm willing to call myself the chair, *tout court,* avoiding the sexist title, but the others think I'd be too tolerant of views they don't like; the Lear syndrome, it's called, and I don't have it. I'm not supposed to know about it, but I do. Larry Petrillo told me; now there's a nice guy, even though he keeps extending the medieval period well into the Renaissance. Anyway, it was certainly going to be Haycock; I don't know who it will be now."

"Lear syndrome?" I hated to ask, but I thought I'd better; it might be a clue. I could have waited and asked Kate—that might have been the sensible thing to do—but he seemed to welcome the question. Anyway, my instinct told me to keep away from the chairman question now; it sounded like a good motive, and I wanted to learn more about it before taking it up.

"No reason you should know about Lear. You're a detective, not a scholar, my dear. I won't ask what you majored in in college. Lear, whether through senility or the compassion of old age, gave his kingdom away to his nasty daughters. You see the relevance."

"Of course. And he didn't give any part to his good daughter, because she wouldn't tell him she loved him.

Sorry to have been so slow in catching on." I'd seen *Lear* once on television, just the beginning, but I didn't see any point in mentioning that.

"You show promise; don't apologize. They're all afraid of nasty women taking over, all except David Lermann; it's the new theoretical lingo he objects to. He thinks anyone who even mentions theory has defiled the language and should be shot. Neither Tony nor Catherine went in for theory in a big way, but they didn't refuse to acknowledge it. Lermann called them illiterate; so did Haycock."

"But I thought only tenured professors came to those faculty meetings."

"Lermann is tenured, even though he's an assistant professor. He got de facto tenure. Somebody in the administration was nodding, and he taught here long enough to get automatic tenure. The old boys were so outraged that they've never given him a promotion. He isn't really stodgy, except about the English language; he hasn't published anything, but the students love him. You'd think he might resent the other tenured men, but no—he's really the sweetest guy in the world. He ought to have been promoted, but around here, no chance."

"It all sounds, well, rather, well, not what you'd expect from college professors." I was really getting nervous, and worrying if maybe the old boy was indeed losing his marbles.

"Don't take it from me," he said cheerfully, reading my mind. "Ask around; find out for yourself. You'll see I'm right."

"I'm sure I will. Who do you think killed Professor Haycock?"

"Just about anybody, I'd say. Nobody around here is very lovable, but Charles took offensiveness to a new level. I'd say your problem in finding the murderer, if any, is going to be a challenging one. Everyone had the opportunity; everyone had a motive; perhaps getting the means wasn't too hard."

"Might he have killed himself?"

"Charles? Never. Besides, if he'd decided to kill himself, he'd have done it so that someone was the obvious suspect. No, I think you can dismiss suicide; the police seem to have done so."

"What was your motive?"

"Easy, my dear. He wanted to be chairman and so did I. I thought with him out of the way, they'd have to settle for me, Lear syndrome or not. I thought the chairmanship would be a nice way to end my long career."

He smiled saying this, and while I was trying to interpret his words, a student came to the door. I stood up and said my farewells.

"Come again anytime, my dear," he said. "Come in, Mr. Franklin; still puzzled by *Hamlet*, are we? What exactly do you find troublesome?"

I left them to it, and went to ask Dawn if anyone else had come back to the office. She told me that Antonia Lansbury was probably still in her office, probably still seeing students.

She was. I waited at the end of the line, making notes and wondering if Professor Longworth was having me on, making me into one of his Shakespearean fools, or if all college departments could possibly be as unpleasant as this one.

CHAPTER FIVE

Come, my friends,
'Tis not too late to seek a newer world.
                              —Tennyson, "Ulysses"

Of course, when I finally got into her office, the first thing I did was look at her legs. She had turned her desk chair sideways, and her long legs were stretched out; she'd kicked her shoes off. I could see that she was tired, and I could see that not only were her legs gorgeous, she was thin and gorgeous all over. Two such women in one case: her and Kate. And she was my age, give or take a year, which made it worse. Kate, at least, had settled well into her fifties and wore glasses to read.

"Do I know you?" she asked. "Have you just signed up for the course?"

I stared at her, really worried. No way do I resemble a college student, here or anywhere else.

She understood immediately why I was puzzled. A good sign, I thought; intelligent lady. She said, "We have alumni who come back to take courses, as auditors," she said. "They not infrequently show up after the courses have begun. I take it you are not an alumna and not an auditor."

"I'm a private investigator," I said. "Hired by members of this department to look into Professor Haycock's murder. I'd very much like to talk to you, if you haven't had too long a day. We could make it tomorrow."

"Hell, it's a change of subject, anyway. I'm tired of T. S. Eliot, who hated Jews and women and wrote great poetry, damn him. Close the door, if you don't mind, and have a seat; I leave the door open to avoid any nonsense from students, but privacy seems to be what we need now."

I wondered what sort of nonsense the students threatened—charges of sexual harassment, or what? I didn't ask. I had enough questions without taking her time to satisfy my personal curiosity. Maybe I'd ask later on. Anyway, I was looking around her office, which was rather barren; there were bookshelves all around the room, but few books.

Noticing my gaze, she said, "I work at home. These are only duplicate texts and a few books I lend to students. I don't do my own work here; this place is just where I hold my office hours. Sorry it's so bleak, which everyone notices, but for me this is not a home away from home."

"I was just talking to Professor Longworth," I explained, "and his office is, well, fixed up, with lots of books, and rugs, and an easy chair and lamps. . . ." My voice trailed off. Actually her office looked a lot more like my office than Professor Longworth's did. His office looked to me as though he was trying to have a life there. My office, even if it wasn't derelict, was just a place to meet with people about business, like hers. I decided, temporarily, to forgive her for being thin.

"Please tell me how I can help you," she said. "This department has been seething with ill feeling for far too long; I didn't expect it to end in someone's death, but in theories and interpretations of literature; that would have been the only way for so much hatred to go. If you see what I mean. I'm afraid we English-lit types get to talking as though everyone lived in books as we do, or like to think we do."

"You mean, in books things that might happen do happen, whereas in life they often don't."

"That's part of it. In Dostoyevsky's *Crime and Punishment*, he wants to kill the pawnbroker, but he doesn't really decide to do it until he happens to hear that her sister will be away that night. A coincidence? In life, yes; in books, no. Because the coincidence was simply the manifestation of his intention; what seem to be coincidences in life are really, in books—anyway, in good books—the confirmation of character and will. And, of course, the sister turns up anyway, and he has to kill her too."

I looked at her. I thought of Kate. There was no doubt these literary types lived in some world where literature was more significant to them than events that had really happened. I guess the point is that literature has some meaning to it, and life often doesn't, although people hire us investigators to prove that it does.

"What caused all the ill feeling in this department?" I asked her. "I know there are probably a lot of reasons, but is there a main reason?"

She stretched her legs out and smiled. "You'll get a different answer from each person you ask. From my point of view, the simplest explanation is that these guys used to rule the roost, and now they're not only expected to share it, and to share it with women, they're also expected to change the way they look at the literature they have always taught, and even to consider writings they have never taught. They don't like being displaced, and they don't like being told they are no longer the final authority on what constitutes the canon. If I were one of them, I might not like it either."

"Are they racists too?" I asked.

"No, or at least not blatantly. They like to congratulate themselves on not being racists. But women; that's turning the whole natural order upside down."

"Aren't there younger men who are not quite so . . . well, so set in their ways?"

"Sure there are. And we've had some great younger

male scholars in this department, but the old guys don't want them, and because they're male there aren't as many of the same questions asked when they're turned down. They prefer the old young men whom they could very well have cloned; men as conservative and in love with old-time values as themselves."

"It's not like that with the police," I said. "The racists are almost as bad as the woman-haters. I bet it's the same in the fire department, not to mention sanitation. Different class of people, I guess."

"Exactly," she said, smiling at me the way she probably smiled at a smart student. "And remember, with professors, particularly in literature, they don't feel quite certain that theirs is a manly profession. If women start swarming all over it, they might actually begin to feel feminized. But all that's general, and probably true of other English departments in other colleges, although ours is a bit extreme. At least I hope so. You probably need to know about particulars." She seemed to be deciding the simplest and quickest way to put it, at least for now.

"These guys," she said, "don't like women; they particularly don't like tenured women—that is, women with power—and they don't want any more of them here. We had a great female assistant professor who was up for tenure—maybe you've already heard something about that." I nodded. "They were so set on getting rid of her they used every crooked and ridiculous trick to keep her from being promoted. I fought for her, which of course made her even less desirable, and women in other departments argued with the administration. The students, who really liked her and knew how much attention she gave them, got up a petition. It was all for naught. They won, but I think in a way they lost. They will probably never admit it to themselves, but that victory cost too much. It certainly left me a lot readier to fight them, particularly Haycock. The muttering on all sides continued. They still have the power, but at the same time they began to see the writing on the wall and were scared. *Not* a happy situation."

"So the assistant professor left?"

"She did. She had another year to go, but she didn't want to stay and they didn't want her to stay, so they gave her a semester's pay as terminal leave and she left."

"Any chance she could have dropped the pills in Professor Haycock's retsina?"

"None. One of her prominent qualifications for promotion was that she was bilingual, French and English; she could read Italian and Spanish as well. She wiped the dust of the United States as well as of this college off her feet and settled down in Paris. She and I communicate via e-mail; she's fine, if disillusioned about academia. But then, aren't we all?"

"It still seems a neat job to me," I said. "You read

most of the time; you talk about what you read, and people have to listen to you; you write about what you read. A lot less dirty than many jobs."

"Granted. And people who agree with you usually add that we get our summers off as well as sabbaticals, a semester every seven years—though that's no longer as automatic as it used to be—and they can't fire you except for the most egregious of reasons. Who's to agree now on what that is? In the old days it was a lovely job on the whole. God knows, I wanted it. But now? It's really nasty, in a way I'm told even business isn't. There's too little money, so dissension over which department gets funds to hire faculty gets more and more bitter. Worst of all, there aren't enough jobs for the Ph.D.'s being produced, and that turns the whole process sour."

"I know something about that," I said, remembering Kate's rendition of the subject.

"What's really ironic is that the administration here and I'm sure elsewhere was in a panic when compulsory retirement for faculty was made illegal. My God, they said, we'll have ninety-year-olds tottering around. Now, those old enough to draw their full pension and social security can't wait to leave. Unfortunately," she added with a shrug, "our 'old boys' are still in their late fifties or just a bit beyond. And the young-old boys are young, damn them."

I'd been taking notes, and now I looked up at her.

"How I do go on," she said, beginning to gather up her papers. "While the others may not be as frank with you, or may be too tired at the end of a long day to be succinct, they'll all agree about the state of the department whether they tell you so or not; only the sides they're on will differ."

"Don't the men get as tired as you by the end of the day?" I asked, partly to make myself a bit less sympathetic.

"If you want a blunt answer, it's no. I may be a better teacher than some of them, but that isn't the point. First of all, I'm the only tenured woman around, although the woman they canned took a lot of the weight of that off me. Then, the students these days are intrigued by feminism, even if all they want to do is sneer at it; they're certainly interested in women and sex. Those students who are gay, men and women, gravitate toward me because I'm expected not to be homophobic, which I'm not. If some senior wants to write a thesis on homosexuality in any work from Chaucer's on, he or she is sent to me. It is handy to assume that feminists understand these things. Well, most of us do, but why don't *they* try a little? Also, I'm on too many administrative committees, put there so they can say there is a woman on board. God, how I really do go on. I actually am very tired. Sorry."

"I'm the one who ought to apologize for keeping you

so late," I said, rising to my feet, tucking away my notebook, and picking up my helmet. "Perhaps we can talk
again sometime—maybe at lunch, when you've only
had to make it through half a day?"

"Anytime," she said. "Unpleasant as the atmosphere
is around here, it will certainly be better when this investigation is over. Have they definitely decided he was
murdered?"

"I think so, though there are far too many loose ends.
Could I ask you just one more question for now?"

"If it's a short one," she said; she was ready to leave
with me, waved me out, and closed her office door behind her, locking it. We walked down the stairs together ("The elevator never comes, though I sometimes
wait for it going up," she explained), and she didn't
even ask me about my helmet. She was either very tired,
or tactful enough to spare what she could guess had become a tiresome question.

"What do you want to know that requires a very short
answer?" she said when we were outside of the building.
The wind had risen, and her hair was blowing. She
pushed it back from her face.

"What do you think of Professor Haycock's"—I groped
for a word—"devotion to Tennyson?"

"That may be a short question"—she laughed—"but
the answer could fill hours, if not days. All I'll say for
now is that if Tennyson were part of the motive in this

investigation, you'd be detecting a different murder: mine."

Waving, she walked off in a determined way. I didn't bother waving back, since she just kept looking ahead; I set off for the parking lot.

The next day I called Dawn first thing in the morning; I wanted the name of one of the "good" young men, one of those Antonia had admired, who had been fired. I wanted, in addition to his name, his current address and his new job, if he had one. If she could find me an assistant professor, late of Clifton College, who was working on the eastern seaboard I would consider myself fortunate. Most of those fired, I gloomily suspected, were now employed in the Midwest, happy perhaps, but distant, too distant for a trip on my motorbike or by commuter train.

But my luck was in. One of the young men fired three years ago had been hired by Rutgers University in New Brunswick, New Jersey, where he also lived. Dawn gave me his home, office, and e-mail address, as well as his phone number. She had been forwarding mail to him until recently, and he still occasionally kept in touch. Profusely thanking Dawn for this information, I asked her again to have dinner with me. "You'll be doing me a favor," I said, before she could protest. "This is not an easy case, and talking to you helps to clear my

mind. What kind of dinner would you like this time?"
I asked.

"Could we go to the same place?" she asked. "It was
delicious and we could talk there; most restaurants are
so noisy." We made a date for a few days hence.

The assistant professor, late of Clifton, now of Rutgers, responded to my call with more enthusiasm than I
anticipated. This case looked like one of those, com-
moner to fiction than life, where the good guys are all
on one side and the baddies are all on the other. This is
not a situation conducive to sharp detective work; one
tends to take sides and to become blinded by fa-
voritism, as though the suspects were on teams.

Richard Fowler, speaking from New Jersey, sounded
so nice it was obvious why Clifton hadn't kept him. He
agreed to meet me in New York ("Any excuse to revisit
that great city is welcome") and told me he was a different man from the one I would have met three years ago
at Clifton.

"Do you garden?" he surprisingly asked. I denied any
such inclination.

"Well," he said, "since settling in New Brunswick,
we've taken up gardening. That is, my partner's taken
it up, and urges me to join in; physical and spiritual
therapy, he calls it. I gave him a gardening book, and he
read me this bit out of it that perfectly describes the

English department at Clifton. The gardening expert's describing something called tickseed—*Coreopsis lanceolata,* officially. No, wait a minute, there is a point to this story. The instructions for growing tickseed might have been internalized by the tenured faculty at Clifton as the way to treat inferiors. Hold on." He must have reached for the book, because he didn't leave the phone. "Tickseed, we are told, 'prefers well-aerated sandy soil with some humus; but the soil should not be too good as the plant produces more leaves than flowers in fertile ground.'* Not too good soil and us growing more leaves than flowers says it all, trust me." We made an appointment to meet the next evening. "Don't worry," he assured me before disconnecting, "I won't confine my evidence to horticultural metaphors."

We arranged to meet the next evening at Knickerbocker's in the Village—booths (I reserved one) and more down-to-earth food than I ate with Dawn. It occurred to me that dinners were playing a bigger part than usual in this investigation, but of course I would count them as legitimate expenses, which they were, when I handed in my account. After all, I was dealing with academics.

* Guido Mogg and Luciano Giugnolini, *Guide to Garden Flowers,* translated by Sylvia Mulcahy (New York: Simon & Schuster, 1983), p. 93.

Once I'd made the appointment with Richard Fowler, I called Kate to see if I could stop in for a chat. I'd more or less gathered that late afternoon was drinky time around the Fansler establishment, and that intriguing chat might be welcome. I had to be careful not to overdo my welcome or to make my remarks less than interesting. But what I had to say to Kate wouldn't be a worry to me this time. She couldn't make it that particular afternoon, she said, but she could usually make it; I shouldn't stop calling, especially since, as I'd seen, she would frankly let me know if it didn't work out. I was feeling a bit let down, but maybe that was because everything about this case was confusing and not exactly getting anywhere.

Richard Fowler was waiting for me outside of Knickerbocker's, leaning against the entranceway. He seemed to recognize me as I walked up, and led me into the restaurant as though this was the very evening in his whole life he had been waiting for. I liked him with an immediacy rare with me when investigating murder cases, though I had to admit it was growing less rare with this case. Still, he seemed so much less tense than the academics I had met so far, less serious, more inclined toward fun or frivolity. They showed us into our booth, and handed us menus.

"I can tell we're going to get on," he said. "I'm gay and you're fat, and we're both lovable. And we both understand that if I'm going to help you figure out who offed dreary old Haycock, it's because I'm against murder in general, not his in particular."

It hardly required my fine investigative eye to discern that he was bursting to tell me what he thought of the English department at Clifton College, and that what he had to say was not likely to be modified either in tone or content. Everyone else I'd met during this case had been so restrained, or anyway so careful, that I felt wonderfully relaxed and hopeful. When the server asked us if we wanted a drink, Fowler said he didn't feel like wine, could he have a vodka martini?

I said sure, he could have whatever he wished, and I would have one too so that we could lift similar glasses to the afterlife of Professor Haycock. He immediately got the message that he could drink all he wanted on the lady detective, but that she would probably stop at one, being as it were in harness. An insightful chap.

"I know," he said to reassure me, "a little buzz is one thing, a cheery fog is quite another; you're working."

"That's it," I said. I'd left the bike at home, as I always do for dinner engagements—what is dinner without some proper liquid accompaniment? With Dawn I could finish my half bottle of wine and keep up with her and her revelations; with Rick, as he asked me to call him, I hadn't a clue what he would say or what I would want to ask, and I was grateful to him for realizing that.

I was feeling a pleasant glow even before our drinks came. Well, why not? Within a few days I had met Kate Fansler and Antonia Lansbury, two women I was able to talk to on a more or less equal basis. Well, not equal, I guess, more from me up to them. This was a first for me. In my work I talked to a lot of men on what you might call a level playing field, but with women I almost always looked down on them at least a little—I admit it—and had to coax what information I wanted out of them with patience and skill that it had taken a lot of time to learn. Most of the women who came to me as clients were in trouble, hadn't ever dealt with a private eye, and were reluctant to come forth with what was actually on their minds. I might feel sorry for them before I was through, I might despise them, but I wouldn't expect to learn much from their particular personalities. Funny that I'd never thought of this before I met Kate and Antonia. Maybe there was something to be said for the academic life. Not, I reminded myself, that the men were likely to turn out to be any special gift or any different from men I'd met up with before.

I gathered my wandering thoughts together as the waiter brought our martinis. We raised our glasses and clinked them together.

"To the passing of the old order," Rick said.

"To the solving of this murder," I said. He might have to live with the old order or the new, but I had a case to get moving on.

"I don't know who did for old Haycock," he said. "If I did I'd tell you. It wasn't me—and you mustn't let that denial make you suspicious of me. I might kill someone; I don't say I wouldn't, and if I became murderous, someone like Haycock would be a likely victim. But I found it easier just to get out."

"Somehow I had the impression things had gotten worse in the last years. Were they always so tense?"

"They sure were, while I was there. Look, baby, the place isn't a university, it isn't famous, it probably isn't even notable. But those old codgers had a nice little setup. They did well by all the little lady students—it used to be all women until ten or fifteen years ago—and all of a sudden, people are questioning the old guys' right to domain."

"Were they sorry to see the place go coed?"

"No, tickled at first. Boys, young men, ho-ho, what we are doing is now significant. But of course the female students just loved listening to the wisdom sprouting from those wise heads, or pretended to. The boys weren't so patient, and the girls weren't either anymore. The women's movement maybe, who knows why, but somehow the nest was beginning to unravel. And then the young faculty got uppity. My dear, the old boys fairly seethed. If I were a sadist, I would have stayed just to see them writhe."

"But you didn't."

"No. I guess it was making me a little tense. My partner . . ."

"The one who's taken up gardening."

"The same. He said I was making him jumpy as hell, and that he wasn't going to sit around and watch me turn into a nervous wreck when I had the chance to move to a better place in every way and one where we could have a house and a garden. I adore New York City—he and I used to live here and I commuted to Clifton—but he's a country lad. So I escaped."

"And you don't miss it a bit?" I added, as we ordered our food and he gestured for another drink.

"I miss the city. One does, if one has learned to love it. New York is a funny place. Living here is either mandatory or forbidden, it seems; there's no middle way, though I'm learning to make do living in New Jersey as well as working there. And I miss Antonia," he said. "I see her from time to time, and I listen with a magnificently sympathetic and knowledgeable ear to her cries of distress, but it's not the same as working together."

"Were you in modern literature too?" I asked. "I'm afraid these fields or areas or whatever you call them aren't as distinct in my mind as they might be."

"They shouldn't be that clear in anyone's. I was an Americanist, actually, hired as one by the Clifton department. But I didn't make any secret of the fact that I was gay, and then queer studies came along. . . ."

"Queer studies?"

"It sounds like an insult to your innocent ears? It isn't; self-named in fact by the practitioners thereof. Anyway, the gay movement had taken on steam, there were some among the student body either already gay or wondering if they might be, or just interested, and of course when a perfectly normal-looking young man asked to write his senior thesis on homosexuality, the old boys flipped. At first they were going to forbid it on the grounds that it wasn't really literature, and then they decided to turn it over to me and Antonia."

"Is Antonia gay too?"

"No, baby, but she's a feminist, and they figured they might as well put all the crazies together. She and I cooperated on directing senior honor theses, became comrades in arms, otherwise known as friends. There're a lot of great people where I am now, but no Antonia. I'd love to get her to move near me. Get yourself a garden, I say, but the very thought of New Jersey sends chills up her spine. It's something I've noticed in a lot of New Yorkers. A bit odd, but who am I to throw stones? Ah, here's our food."

I asked for iced tea, not without having a fierce inner battle with myself over wine. I was happy listening to Rick, and I would have liked another drink. I couldn't remember another case where I seemed so often to be wishing I wasn't investigating and could just relax; I worried about it. But not half as much as I worried when Rick really got going on the English department at Clifton College, and the story of him and Antonia.

CHAPTER SIX

I scribbled notes while Rick talked, writing with one hand and occasionally scooping up mouthfuls of food with the other. It was a technique I had fully developed. The notes I took on such occasions rarely turned out to be important, but taking them was necessary to ensure concentration on what I was hearing. If I just listened, it was possible I would let something significant slip by me; taking down the sense of what was being said meant I didn't miss much. It worked, at least for me.

Some detectives pride themselves on having a meticulous memory and perfect recall. Maybe they do, although I doubt it; and even if they can rely on their unerring memory today, who knows what tricks it may play tomorrow? Some P.I.'s use tape recorders, but I scorn that. It's like copying some essential document instead of reading it. Tapes are okay for interviews, but no good for detection, not unless you want some sort of legal record, and then the courts will probably throw it out. I use tapes only to bully reluctant husbands who think there's no proof with which their wives can nail them for adultery; sometimes I find that hearing their own voices saying what they denied having said pushes them over the edge.

I took notes as Rick talked, stopping now and then to wave for another martini and going into more and more digressions, which is to say more and more details. I didn't interrupt often, and then only with a question to refuel his energy for compulsive talking. Not that I blamed him for the way he felt about Clifton; and I thought he'd certainly been smart to get out and move away. But at the same time, I could tell that the likelihood of his forgetting, or forgiving, or getting over the Clifton experience was not great.

He spoke of the dynamic of relationships in the English department there. Sick, he called them, and I could hardly doubt it. The "old boys," as he dubbed them, meaning everyone who had been there since forever, joined ranks to defeat any new appointment or promotion to tenure they found in any way threatening, which Rick said was all of them. They promoted and hired only clones of themselves. At the same time, he insisted, these older types didn't exactly like each other much either, and bickering went on between them, at meetings and in the corridors, punctuated by insincere greetings to whoever was passing. One of them, according to Rick, would shout out, "Fine," if anyone seemed to be greeting him, although he was too deaf to know what the greeting was or if anyone was asking him how he felt.

Meanwhile, he and Antonia, and three of the four assistant professors, including the one who was away this year, had joined into a group supporting one another, and letting off steam at regular intervals. He and Antonia and the assistant professor, Catherine Dorman, who had been turned down for tenure, were the closest. Rick's partner, Frank, had gotten to enjoy the group as well. The four of them often met at Rick and Frank's apartment to discuss department conditions and possible maneuvers. Well, Rick said, Catherine was gone now, and he and Frank lived in New Jersey, but he sure as hell missed Antonia, seeing her on a regular basis, talking with her, laughing together.

"What did you laugh at, mainly?" I asked. He was getting a little repetitive, and I thought concentrating on some particulars was not a bad idea.

"Tennyson," Rick said. "Tennyson, and Haycock's idiotic books on him. Harold Nicolson, in a book written in the Twenties, had referred to Tennyson's 'polluted muse,' and Haycock had written volumes, absolute volumes, refuting, or trying to, that hideous phrase. Antonia looked it up and found that Nicolson was actually quoting a review on Tennyson's early work; it also referred to Tennyson's 'feminine feebleness'—never will I forget that phrase. Obviously Haycock refused even to quote it in anger; the idea of Tennyson as feminine, let alone feeble, was more than he could countenance. And should anyone suggest that Tennyson and Hallam had loved not wholly in the pure way of manly men—well, I need hardly tell you what old Haycock would have thought of that. Actually, he might have burst a blood vessel and saved whoever did it from murdering him."

I looked puzzled, and I was. "You think it all sounds mad?" Rick asked.

"Not mad, perhaps, but hardly what I imagined academics went on about. They sound more like kids arguing over the relative skill of baseball players."

"Of course they do. You've seen too many professors in movies, Woody, my love. Haycock had given his whole working life to Tennyson, he liked to think of himself as the world's authority on Tennyson, and he suspected that Antonia was trying to take Tennyson, which is to say his life, away from him."

"Was she?"

"No, of course not. If he'd been a little more sensible about everything, including women and Tennysonian criticism, he'd have played around with it, and everyone would have been happy. But instead he fought Antonia and everything she stood for, including, alas, Catherine Dorman, who, one has to admit, joined Antonia in whooping up the Bloomsbury view of Tennyson."

"Bloomsbury?" I said, sneaking a look at my watch. Please God, I said to myself irreverently, don't make whatever he plans to say about Bloomsbury important; I was too tired. But tired or not, it was clear Rick was getting to the heart of the matter, and I had better pay attention. I signaled the waiter for coffee, and looked at Rick with what I hoped would pass for eager anticipation.

"Decaf?" the waiter asked, responding to my summons.

"Certainly not," I barked at the poor man. "Perhaps you can double the caffeine."

"Getting sleepy?" Rick asked, not quite mockingly. Thanking what powers there be that I hadn't drunk much, I denied this charge with vigor, and urged him on to explain what he meant by Bloomsbury.

"They were a group of clever people—geniuses, some of them—in England between the wars. Who they were doesn't matter. Virginia Woolf was perhaps the most important. She and her sister Vanessa Bell, an artist, and various relatives and friends, liked to put on plays. Virginia wrote them, Vanessa designed them, and they were produced in Vanessa's studio. The cast of this particular play included Duncan Grant, who was an artist, Vanessa's longtime lover, a homosexual, and the father of Angelica, Vanessa's daughter, who was in the play, together with Vanessa's son Julian, by Clive Bell, her husband, and Virginia's nieces, the daughters of her brother Adrian."

My eyes were rolling. Perhaps I had overlooked a few of his drinks. "Were these people in the English department?" I asked.

"You haven't been listening carefully," Rick said, sounding not the least drunk. "Although I admit it is confusing at first."

"I should think it would be confusing forever," I said nastily.

"Never mind all that. I'm telling you about Bloomsbury, which included the aforementioned as well as others. They didn't go in for conventional sexual morality, but that's not the point right now. The point is that this group put on a play called *Freshwater*, which had Tennyson in it as a character, mocked—lovingly mocked, but mocked. Virginia had grown up with 'Maud,' and was only joshing at what she loved, but Haycock could hardly be expected to understand that. It increased his hatred of Antonia and her part in the play, and everything and everyone she touched."

"Who is Maud?" I said, though I hardly dared to ask.

"Oh, Jesus," Rick cried—a name I never evoke in anger. I'm not religious, but there is such a thing as respect. I frowned.

"Sorry," Rick said. " *'Maud'* is a poem by Tennyson; a famous poem: 'Come into the garden, Maud, / For the black bat, night, has flown, / Come into the garden, Maud, / I am here at the gate alone.' Those are the lines quoted in the play. Antonia and Catherine and Frank and I put it on once, for an audience of friends; we had a few others in the cast, of course."

"Of course," I said.

"Don't you even know *'Alice'?*" he asked, as though suddenly considering whether or not he had been wasting his time, and whether the people who hired me ought to have their heads examined. " 'She's coming! cried the Larkspur, I hear her footstep, thump, thump, thump, along the gravel walk,' " he quoted happily.

"Rick," I said. "Could we put this into context for a simple soul like me? It's getting late, and we should think of leaving. Could we sum it all up?" The great thing about New York restaurants is that people go on eating all evening, the later the better, so the waiters don't start glaring at you if you stay awhile. They'd like new customers and new tips, but when leaving a tip I always take into account how long I've been hanging around taking up the table; it's only fair.

"To sum up," he said pompously, "the Moderns do not think Tennyson is the greatest thing in literature; in fact, they count him as rather dull. Harold Nicolson even thought he was pretty awful, except for some of his lyrics. Personally, I like some of Tennyson; I used to memorize 'Ulysses' as a child. Well, I won't quote it now; and then there's 'Tithonus.' That's where Aldous Huxley got the title, 'After many a summer dies the swan.' "

"Rick," I said, dire threats evident in my voice.

"Haycock thought Antonia and Catherine, being Modern and playing around with *Freshwater*, were, so to speak, pissing in his and Tennyson's tea. It was just one more thing to add to his hatred of women in academia, any literature later than Queen Victoria, and all those who didn't think Tennyson was what poetry was all about. I think that even the other old boys got a bit weary of Tennyson and the other Victorians Haycock went on and on about. Ruskin is okay, but he was a bit tiresome about Whistler."

"Rick!"

"Damn it, Woody, you asked for the context. That's the context! He was a perfectly dreadful person. Was he dreadful enough to induce someone to drop serious poison into his drink? I wouldn't have thought so, but then, someone did, didn't they? I've no doubt most of those in the department would like to blame Antonia, but killing people isn't Antonia's way. Don't believe me on this. Talk to all her other friends. Look, I've got an idea: Antonia was friendly with a woman who used to be dean of the faculty at Clifton. She'd had enough before Haycock got knocked off, so she isn't a suspect, but she'd be a good person to talk to for the whole picture, so to speak. Here, I'll give you her phone number."

He took out one of those small electronic appointment books, telephone directories, and keeper of all secrets as far as I know. The thought of something electronic wiping out all my appointments and notes is more than I can contemplate. I'll take up using one when paper and pens are no longer available.

"Here we are," he said. He read me off her full name—Elaine Kimberly—and her address and telephone number. I wrote them down and waved for the bill. I had every intention of calling her first thing in the morning, but then I had a horrible thought. "She isn't a literary type, is she?" I asked with more passion than tact.

Rick laughed. "Not exactly; something in the classics line, I think. I doubt she'll have any views on Tennyson or Bloomsbury. Anyway, deans give all that academic stuff up when they start deaning. No time for mere academic pursuits; time only for academic politics. I think you'll like her."

We parted outside. He offered to talk to me again anytime. I thanked him and said I'd be in touch, which maybe I would be when I recovered from this evening. I couldn't imagine why they'd hired me to find Haycock's murderer and, more to the point, why I'd taken the damn job. Oh, well, there was always the dean. I had high hopes of the dean.

Dean Kimberly still lived in New Jersey, in one of those upper-class areas that somehow fail to conform to the rather tacky impression people seem to have of New Jersey. Not that I was overwhelmed by the elegance, mind you. The neighborhood didn't strike me as that different from the elegant parts of Westchester. For my money, suburbia is suburbia until you're at least far enough from New York City for all the natives to be Republicans with opinions of New York varying from unlivable to sinister. Still, her house, when I reached it, looked inviting: land, big trees, no impression of anything being manicured, and with a large dog lying on the stoop. Not a Saint Bernard, but huge, black with a white face. It rose to its feet as I roared up on my bike, but didn't bark. It just kept me covered, as it were. Big dogs figure they can handle it and don't need to arouse the troops; I've noticed that.

She must have heard the bike, because she came to

the door and waited, with a pleasant air of greeting, for me to dismount and shed my helmet. I took to her immediately, suburb or not. We went into her front hall, the dog with us, where I left my helmet and jacket and followed her into the kitchen.

"I thought you might like a cup of coffee or tea," she said. I told her coffee would be fine, and like every other nut in the world—strictly my own opinion—she started to grind coffee beans. We said nothing during the short racket, and nothing further while the coffee machine gurgled away. She had one of those coffee-brewing gadgets attached to the wall. Detecting, I concluded that she was a devoted coffee drinker. I requested milk and sugar when asked; I would have preferred cream or half-and-half, but nobody keeps that sort of thing around these days; it's a no-no. Too bad, really, because coffee with cream is simply delicious.

"Would you rather drink it here or in the living room?" she asked. "The chairs are more comfortable in there."

"I always like sitting around a table," I said, settling down. In my experience conversation goes better around a table; people relax more and when I make notes I've got something ready to be leaned on. She sat down opposite me and sipped her coffee—black, of course. Someday those research types are going to discover that cholesterol is essential to health, and the effects of avoiding it downright deleterious. You can bet on it.

"Rick called me," she said. "He told me you want to talk about the college and particularly the English department. I should warn you that I'm not your best source for information on the English department, although by the time I left I did have the impression that it was in pretty bad shape. Do you remember the Clinton impeachment hearings in Congress, in the House?"

"Definitely. Very partisan," I added, suspecting that was the point she wanted to make. "The Republicans were out to get him, no other considerations allowed."

"Exactly. That's what had happened to the English department by the time I quit. The more established professors were against any new approaches to literature, and did not want even to consider them. For instance, there was one of the older members, Daniel Wanamaker, who was chair of the department, a man I liked and had a great deal of respect for; we had served together on a number of policy-setting committees. I hear he's retiring this year. I thought him honorable, which he certainly had been. But when I pointed out to him that the department had blatantly rigged a vote on a new hire—the evidence having been given me, as dean, by a more forward-looking member of the department—he simply shrugged. It shook me up."

"Is that why you left the college?"

She rose to get herself another cup of coffee. I shook my head when she looked to see if I wanted another. She wasn't a woman to waste words on persuasion, which I liked about her. Try as I might—and I do try, I really do—not to be swayed by first impressions, all the same I get them and believe them. I'm aware that dishonest types know how to make a good impression, but I like to think I can see through that. I can't, of course; no one can, not all the time. But you can't help responding to people. It's just important to be ready to shift views if required.

"It was just a small piece of why I left. Mostly why I left is personal and probably hasn't anything to do with your investigation. Or not much. It is true that the tone, the spirit of the whole college had, in my opinion, badly deteriorated. I'd say that the attitude of that professor in the English department, representing the dominant force there, was repeated throughout the administration. I was fighting a lonely battle; I was fighting it as a woman, which made it harder; and one day I just decided it was enough. I walked out."

She smiled, anticipating my question. "No, I don't mean I got up from my desk, left, and never came back. I handed in my resignation and finished out the year. They wanted me to stay until they found a new dean, but I wasn't having that. Either the new dean would be a creature in their own image, whom I would dread meeting, or, if not, I would have to warn the poor slob not to take the job."

"Have you always lived here? It must be quite a commute from the college."

"I had a small apartment near the college, and stayed there Tuesday, Wednesday, and Thursday nights. This is where my home was and obviously still is. This is where I've lived ever since my divorce, after our children were grown and out in the world. Surely that can't have anything to do with Professor Haycock's murder. It's a while since I've even seen anyone from the college."

"Did you know anything about the fight to promote that young woman whom they succeeded in turning down? That seems to have been a major event in the life of the English department—the culminating event, so to speak."

"I knew something about it because I'm a friend of Antonia's. We used to meet from time to time and talk about the department's situation; she was very upset about that decision and about the way it had been handled. Sometimes she'd drive out here for a cup of coffee—just like you. Would you like a cookie, by the way? Have one. I made them." She pushed the plate toward me; I'd been eyeing them in the middle of the table, and trying to avoid glancing at them too often.

"Do you live here all alone?" I asked. I knew she did,

but it pays sometimes to ask questions to which you know the answer, as opposed to suspecting the answer. People respond to personal questions differently, and how they respond tells you about them; at least, I find it does.

"Very much alone," she said. "Look, Ms. Woodhaven—"

"Woody," I said. "Everyone calls me Woody."

"Perhaps you should know the sort of peculiar woman I am before you put any stock into what I have to say about the college. Because I'm a very odd person indeed; some might even say madly eccentric."

I looked interested, which I was, and nodded. I decided to take one more cookie and stop thinking about them. My appetite, if sufficiently indulged, reaches a point where it's willing to give up its demands. She smiled, having followed my reasoning about the cookie. I liked her for that, and got on my guard.

"The truth is, I probably welcome the chance to tell someone I don't know how it was all worked out in my mind. I haven't talked about this in a long time, and not often then. You see, leaving my job wasn't all I left. I sometimes think I would have stayed there, at the college, if it had been a place I could feel allegiance to and want to be part of. But since it clearly wasn't that, it had to go, along with everything else that was supposed to be central to my life."

"Like your marriage," I suggested, just to help her along.

"No. My marriage ended years before all this, when the children were in college. I'm in my sixties, you know." I did know, but there was no point in saying so.

"Here's the part that will probably shock you, and make you think I'm hardly a credible, or at any rate, an altogether reasonable witness. My children, with their children, came here a few years ago for Christmas. They had always come, but this turned out to be the last time. I didn't mind preparing the food; I like to cook. I had bought and trimmed a tree, and I was acting as though Christmas were an occasion I was bound to enjoy. And when the children were young, my husband and I, and in those days our parents, did enjoy it. Perhaps it's truer to say it didn't occur to us not to enjoy it; it was something we did. It was a natural way to celebrate Christmas.

"On this particular Christmas, the grandchildren were especially noisy and unpleasant, and so were their parents—my children. I didn't say anything, but I suppose my displeasure was evident. The day finally came to an end with me straightening up here and returning my home to the way I liked it: quiet, tidy, with all my things where I had left them, or wanted them, and with no thought of anyone else in my space. It seems odd to me now that I had never before felt quite so overcome with delight at being alone here, rather like a cat purring, that kind of contentment. We don't know, of course," she added, "that cats purr because they are contented, but that's how it sounds and so that's what it means for us."

I nodded; I liked the way she didn't make claims she didn't feel entitled to. I liked the fact that she was thinking as she spoke, not just repeating a long-practiced rendition of resentment. So far, anyway.

She got up to get us more coffee. It was delicious coffee, but if I drank much more I would have to pee, which would interrupt the session. I let her pour it, all the same. I'm not as disciplined for a detective as I should be, as I'm the first to admit.

She sat down again and continued. "I don't quite know what I would have felt if that had been all there was to it, but my children, both of them, wrote to tell me that they resented the way I had treated their children. I had not responded to the little ones' request to watch a video with them. I had to keep an eye on the food cooking, of course, but the truth, which I was determined to face, was that I didn't want to watch that video, and I didn't particularly want to watch the children watching it, which was supposed to offer me, as a natural grandmother, extraordinary pleasure. I didn't think that I had to indulge my grandchildren, just because it was expected of me."

She looked out of the window. "You know," she said, "something snapped, or perhaps I should say fell into place. I don't want to offer you an extended disquisition on a woman's life, and how it is made to seem that she really wants what she has, how she believes she has what she wants, and, if she has any secret desires, which are against all the forces of her culture, she hardly dares to face them." She paused for a moment. "At the time, after that Christmas I mean, Antonia sent me a sentence from Simone de Beauvoir's autobiography. Beauvoir had written of some woman that 'she was going to mingle with the others, she was going to submit to their conventions and their lives, betraying the "real life" she had glimpsed in her solitude.' Well, I did it the other way around; I had begun by submitting to the conventions, and now I was going to glimpse my solitude. Antonia is a good friend, and a great supplier of relevant quotations.

"I thought maybe I should never have had children, never pretended to enjoy family holidays, never in fact become a dean to earn enough money to support the children and get them through college."

"What would you have done? Stayed a professor?" I really wanted to understand.

"I don't know. That was in the past, and I was a different woman then. All I could know was what I wanted now, and what I wanted now was absolutely clear. To begin with the really shocking bit, I discovered I didn't want to see my children again. Isn't that frightful? I actually admitted to myself that neither they nor their company brought me any pleasure. I had done all I should have done for them; I was the best mother I could be. Now that was over. I sent them letters saying that I didn't think we ought to meet or communicate anymore. I was careful to state plainly that this was not a response to their letters but simply the truth of how I felt. Believe me, Woody"—and she smiled at me—"it is a terribly shocking idea that a mother might not care to go on seeing her children. A man might do that, just barely, but a woman—she must be mad! Well, maybe I was." She looked up at me, as though expecting an expression of distaste.

"I'm not shocked," I said. "I don't want children and don't like them. For one thing, I can't understand why, if there is more than one of them, they scream all the time. At least those that I meet do." I don't know why I wanted to tell her that, but since it was true I thought it might indicate that I could sympathize.

I decided to put it another way. "We have families, and we owe them support and nurturing"—I didn't want to say *affection*—"for a certain amount of time. But why must it be forever if we don't want it to be? Children not liking their parents is just to be expected; parents not liking their children is harder to swallow, I guess."

"Yes," she said. "And the relief was enormous. As though a heavy weight had been lifted from me, as though . . . well, let me put it this way: I've had a cataract operation—I'd been nearsighted, and suddenly this late in life I am able to see without glasses—that's what this decision about the children felt like. It seemed a miracle. Everything else followed from that; I did what I wanted; I made a routine for my day and followed it; I found work I wanted to do."

She saw my question. "I had been a professor of classics. When I began, gender was not a subject anyone discussed. I started reading the Greeks again, and was struck by how central women were in Greek drama, although they were without any power in their society. Why is that? I asked myself. Of course, other critics had noticed the same thing, but that just made my work more exciting. In short, the college, my children, the need to worry about what I wear vanished—E. M. Forster had one of his characters say, 'Mistrust all enterprises that require new clothes.' "

"Did Antonia tell you about that?" I asked.

"Yes, I think she did, long ago. I've always remembered it, though I couldn't tell you when or where he said it."

"Maybe I'll ask her," I said.

She nodded, but she was still thinking about the great change she had brought into her life. "I like conversation," she said, "and can't bear people untalented in that way. Am I ever lonely? That's what I'm often asked. Yes, sometimes I'm lonely, but never as lonely as I was in my marriage, or in the company of my grown children. Here's a minor thing that may seem silly: when I want to watch something on television, I watch it, I can sink into it, nothing draws me away. I don't have to explain why I'm watching some absurd program, as I had to do with my children when they were visiting. I don't watch frivolous programs often, but when I do, it's bliss to just do it, as if it were a sin, really!"

I didn't know what to say. I felt the same about living alone, but because I hadn't married, and didn't look like the sort who'd been overwhelmed with offers from men to shack up with them, no one considered my happy solitude peculiar. It was one of the advantages of not marrying I hadn't exactly realized before. Just then, a cat door I hadn't noticed swung inward and a large cat entered the kitchen.

"Time for the cat to eat," she said, getting up to prepare a dish of food. The cat jumped into a chair and watched her, cleaning itself to pretend it wasn't watching. I do like cats. Someday I'll get one, or maybe two so they can keep each other company when I'm not there.

"What about the dog?" I asked. "He's beautiful." The dog had been lying on the floor, beating the floor with his tail when either of us looked his way.

"Thank you," she said. "He's a Bernese mountain dog—a gift, actually. I'd never have acquired a pure-bred dog on my own, but I do admire his beauty. He's a good old chap." And she bent down, once the cat had begun eating, and stroked the dog's head. "He eats with me," she said. "Dinnertime."

Was this a hint? I glanced at my watch. "I know I should be going," I said, "but I did have one or two more questions."

"About the English department?"

"Well, yes, but also about what you told me. It's none of my business, I know, but don't you ever see your children? You were happy for them just to vanish from your life?"

"Don't apologize for asking. I told you about myself. You've a right to questions. Yes, I do see my children, but not together and not here or in their homes. I dine with them in neutral territory—that is, restaurants— one at a time, just the two of us. I find that there is real communication, that we can enjoy conversation, proba-bly because neither of us is in a situation that tends toward irritation. I wish I'd thought of it earlier." I must have looked an additional question, because she answered it, smiling at me. "Yes, I see my grandchildren too, in the same way. It began when my granddaughter telephoned me and asked if *we* could have a meal in a restaurant. We did, and it was a revelation. She behaved wonderfully and we actually talked to one another. With her family and her cousins, she—well, it's as you said: they scream all the time. Now, what else can I tell you about Clifton College?"

I pulled my thoughts together and concentrated on the task at hand, as I ought to have been doing long since. "Did you ever imagine the situation in the English department could lead to murder? To that much hatred?"

"We sophisticated, so-called literary types never imagine that anything could lead to murder. So I didn't imagine it. But if you put the question, 'Were there to be a murder in that department, who would be the victim,' I would have said Haycock without a second thought. My professor friend who shrugged was not only letting illegalities pass, he was telling me that he didn't want even to have to consider what Haycock was doing to the department. Which doesn't mean the murder didn't astonish me; it did. But not as much as if it had been someone else who died. They are, I take it, sure it's murder and not some sort of mistake?"

"Definitely sure," I said. "What sort of person was Haycock? I mean, how would you describe him?"

"I already have," she said. "He was like those Congressmen we mentioned, the ones who hated Clinton and didn't care what they did to the country, the ones who couldn't believe they weren't in the right, despite all the signs to the contrary, and despite all the damage they were doing to long-established institutions. Haycock was a fanatic, a person who was so sure he was right in his convictions that he could consider no evidence to the contrary. And don't ask me who I think killed him. Anyone at his house that day could have done it, as I understand it." She looked questioningly at me, and I nodded confirmation. Any one of them could have done it, and I wasn't a bit closer to guessing who did it than she was. "But remember," she said, "I wasn't a member of the department and don't know all that went on inside it."

I got to my feet and so did she. "Take another cookie for the road," she said. I complied without argument. I gave her my card and wrote my home number on the back of it, something I seemed to be doing lately. I'd given one to Rick too, and to Antonia. And to Kate.

"If you think of anything else, however insignificant, do let me know," I said. "And thanks for the coffee and the cookies and especially for the conversation. I liked that."

I wanted to say it had meant a lot to me to hear that a mother could feel that way. I'd suspected it, but no one had ever spoken of it so frankly. But that didn't seem the right thing for a private eye to say, so I didn't. She and the dog came to the door to see me off.

I shook her hand and patted the dog. "Say goodbye to the cat," I said, "and thanks for everything." Then I roared off.

CHAPTER SEVEN

I arrived back at the office later than I had hoped. The Lincoln Tunnel was backed up, as though half of New Jersey had decided to visit New York. Going out, I had sailed through: no toll to leave New York, double toll to return. I wondered how many people had left the city for free and never returned. I bet a lot of New Yorkers think they'll get away with that, but come back in the end.

Arriving sweaty and irritable, I found Octavia getting ready to call it a day. "Oh, good," she said when I walked in, "I won't have to leave you a note. Donald Jackson's called several times. He seemed eager to talk to you. Here's his number." She handed me a piece of pink telephone message paper and waved goodbye. I went into my office, slung my helmet into a corner, dropped into my chair, and dialed the number. Some days seem to jolt you around more than others. As it turned out, this wasn't the end of the day's bumpy schedule.

Donald Jackson sounded glad to hear from me. I know what a relief it is to finally get hold of someone who never seems around when you want them.

"Why the hell don't you get a cell phone?" he demanded. "Your secretary said you were in New Jersey, which is where I was hoping to meet with you as soon as possible. Now you'll have to come back; it's important. Trust me, you'll be glad you returned."

"Couldn't you tell me about it over the phone?" I asked rather sheepishly.

"No. We need a long powwow. I have new stuff about our case." I really liked that *our*. No policeman I had ever met up with would have said that. "Get back on your bike and come on out here. Same diner, same menu; you said you liked it."

"I'll have a long wait even at the New York end this time of the day," I said. "Will tomorrow do?"

"It will do, but tonight will do better. Look, Woody, go to Penn Station, get on a train, and I'll meet you at the station. Later, you do the same thing in reverse, having had a couple of beers and maybe something stronger. Don't object. I've got the train schedule right here."

So after dealing with a few matters that ought to have been decided yesterday, and after washing up and combing my hair and trying to make myself look a bit more together, I left for the train station. I felt I could use a drink and some food. I rather liked the thought of seeing Don again, and anyway, I was a private eye and this was the sort of thing private eyes do. I've never admitted it to anyone, but I still have to cheer myself on that way. I left a note for Octavia to find in the morning, saying, *Get me a cell phone, damn it. You win.* Octavia had been after me to get a cell phone for months now. I didn't like the thought of being rung up on my bike or anywhere else, really; I know, I could always turn the damn thing off, but then why bother getting one? Technology was moving right along, too fast for me.

I had the time to walk up to Penn Station and catch the next train. I thought how right Elaine Kimberly was about living alone. Solitude meant I didn't have to explain to anyone why, having just come from New Jersey, I was going back there instead of coming home to supper as expected. Accounting to someone else for your time was the pits; I didn't even have a cat to worry about.

Donald Jackson met me as he said he would, in what I took to be an unmarked police car. Or maybe it was his; I didn't bother asking. Once we had settled down in the diner, and had ordered food and beer, he sat back with a big grin. "You'll never guess the news I have for you," he said.

"I won't even try." I smiled. I liked being there, I liked the hamburger I was eating, I liked looking at him looking pleased with himself. "Let's hear it."

"When the police arrived at the Haycock house, shortly after the ambulance, most of the party was still there, milling around and tut-tutting. The names and addresses of all those present were taken and filed with the usual police report. As you know, Haycock's son was blaming the widow, and we had to wait for the post-mortem, and with one thing and another, including the investigation moving over to the college, I didn't go back to that list of those present the day of the murder until recently. I sent a crew out to question everyone on the list and to get from each person his or her recollection of who had been there, who they had seen even for a minute."

"Good idea," I said to encourage him. "And . . ."

"And, when I put it all together I discovered there'd been a few more folks there than we had figured on." I nodded, urging him along. "Two of them were particularly interesting, because they stayed just for a moment and had left before the death. One was an ex-dean of the college named Elaine Kimberly, and the other was a guy named Frank something, whom we couldn't place at all but who turned out to live with Richard Fowler, late of Clifton College, who hadn't come to the party and hadn't been invited."

I decided to postpone thinking about Richard Fowler's friend until later. It was Elaine Kimberly's name that grabbed me. Don saw the look on my face and said, "What? Tell me, for Pete's sake."

"I spent this afternoon with Elaine Kimberly," I said. "This very afternoon."

"I know that. Your secretary told me. I take it she didn't happen to mention that she'd been at the Haycock shindig."

"Not only didn't she mention it; she diverted me with stories of her major life decisions, tales about her children, solitude, all of it gripping as hell and maybe even true, but leading me far away from any idea that she was at the party or even knew much about Haycock. Damn it to hell! I don't know, Don. Maybe I'm in the wrong line of work. I thought I could see into people, and I let myself be led up the garden path by an ex-dean."

"Now, hold on, Woody. Don't be so hard on yourself. How were you to know she'd been there? If someone who was there hadn't been surprised to see her, and mentioned it when asked, we'd never have known."

"She didn't want it known; she hoped it never would

be. So what you're saying is, she's probably the one who dropped the poison into his Greek wine."

"I'm just saying she may be. She at least knew Haycock. What was that Frank person doing there?"

"You haven't asked him?"

"That's for you to do," he said. "You're the private eye."

"You mean you're not going to interview either of them?"

"We'll have to, eventually. I'm giving you first innings."

"Okay," I said, after some thought. "I like this diner, I like this hamburger, but I still don't see why you couldn't have told me that on the phone."

He smiled. "Because that's not the big news. The big news is that Haycock's widow is back in town—in between travels, I gather—to do her laundry and flip through her mail, and she's willing to talk to me, but only tonight. We can't stop her from leaving as long as she stays in the country. I thought you might like to be in on that."

I would have kissed him, but the booth's table was too wide for that, and I wasn't the right build to slip across it. I did wonder what made him so considerate of me, but the answer lay somewhere in his and Reed's past, and I didn't expect ever to find out.

"We'd better go now, if you can pass up dessert; I'll buy you some later. She's staying at a motel."

"It's my turn to pay," I said firmly, and did. "You can buy dessert later," I added, in case he thought I was being rigid or self-righteous.

"Fine by me," he said as we went out to his car.

The widow Haycock was staying in what Don told me was the best motel in town. To prove this, it called itself a hotel, which seemed to mean either that it was a hotel with motel places to park or a motel with hotel-type service. She agreed to receive us in her room, which was a good idea; any conversation in the so-called lounge area might easily have become public.

She had a largish room, with a huge bed and a table with two chairs around it. Don waved us women to the table and then sat on the end of the bed. He took out a notebook and looked serious, a look designed, I decided, to counter any suggestion that the bed was other than a chair.

"Let's start at the beginning," he said. "When did you decide to go away before your husband's party, and why?"

"You mean the fatal party," she said. "I went because I couldn't stomach watching him swell up with pride as all his acolytes paid him tribute. He hated the thought of retiring; he had to, because of his heart, but he wanted all the demonstrations he could arrange to prove the great respect and love in which he was held. I thought the whole thing best avoided."

"Mrs. Haycock," I intervened at this point. Don looked about ready to make this a duet, so to speak, and I thought a woman-to-woman question might not be amiss. But she interrupted me.

"Please don't call me Mrs. Haycock. I never took his name; my name is, and was, Cynthia Burke. I know what you want to ask, my dear." She smiled at me. "Why did I marry the brute, what made him a brute, and am I glad he's dead?"

I had to keep my mouth from dropping open. "I know," she continued, "you wouldn't have put it that crudely, but if we're going to cover enough ground tonight—I'm definitely leaving for California tomorrow—I thought we had better get to the point."

I nodded my agreement and encouragement.

"Why did I marry him? I was young, foolish, and eager to ally myself with an intellectual, believe it or not. I liked studying and school, I came from a family that thought all that sort of thing snobbish rot, and I thought marrying him would be a coup on several levels. How wrong can you be?"

"Plenty of women marry the wrong man," Don said. "This one does seem, from your point of view, a little more wrong than usual."

"You can say that again. I knew he was stuck on Tennyson—Lord Alfred, and all his gummy works. But I didn't know he actually believed that Tennyson was right on all issues, especially women and the natural order of the sexes. Give me a break!"

" 'He for God, she for the god in him,' " Don surprisingly said.

"Exactly! Not that I ever actually heard that quote. Is that Tennyson?"

"Probably not," Don said. "It just came to my mind." I made a mental note to ask Kate if it was Tennyson. If it was Tennyson, Cynthia would probably have had it quoted to her.

"Listen, honey," she said, echoing my thoughts, "if he'd have quoted anything from Lord Alfred that short on that subject, believe me, I'd remember it. 'Man to command and woman to obey.' I mean, what century did he think he was living in?"

"Did his sons agree with him on that subject?" Don asked.

"If so, they weren't dumb enough to say so. They disliked me on sight, and never gave me the benefit of any doubt. Ever. They just thought I'd married him to hoist myself up in the world—which wasn't altogether untrue—and that I bumped him off to get into his insurance and out of his bed. Well, I'm not a murderer, and I don't like being called one."

"I think the fact that you were well away at the time clears you," Don said. I wasn't so sure of that, but held off saying so.

"I'm really grateful," Cynthia said, "to whoever at that college sent the letter saying it was them. It really let me off the hook, since up to that time I was the only suspect in sight; anyway the only one with a motive."

"It does seem that a lot of his colleagues didn't care for him much either," I said. I glanced over at Don to see if he minded me saying that, but he only changed the subject.

"About the drug that killed him—I gather you knew about it, its uses and its dangers."

"Sure I did. He made such a point about it so often that a bug on the wall must have known its uses and the dangers."

"But you never thought of giving him a larger, fatal dose?"

"No, I didn't, and you can believe it or not; that's up to you. I don't say I never thought of giving him a good smack across his smirking face, but what I really thought of was getting out of there, away from him and his children. Can you imagine naming a kid Hallam because Tennyson had the hots for some guy a hundred years ago?"

"You were planning to leave your husband?" I asked in a formal-sounding way, raising my pencil to make a note. This interview had startled me at first, but now it was falling more into pattern—the pattern of all women who had married the wrong man and deeply regretted it. Most of them took a little longer than this one to spill it all out, but otherwise there was nothing new here.

"Leave him and divorce him. I was prepared to make a nasty case of it if he didn't split the proceeds with me evenly. That's what makes my supposed motive so stupid. With a divorce settlement I'd have gotten half; now I just get the income until I croak, except for his social security and medical benefits, which I would have been entitled to anyway. I know according to Hallam I was supposed to have dropped the fatal drug into that horrible stuff he drank before the party, but I didn't."

"We know that," Don said. "There are a lot of witnesses to the uncorking of the bottle. Of course, it could have been recorked, but that takes a certain kind of expertise."

"Well, I wouldn't have corked or recorked that crap if you had paid me; he made me taste it once. 'Like the pines of Greece,' he said, or something of the sort. I like sweet drinks, like crème de menthe and cream sherry; nothing wrong with that I can see, but he thought it just showed how tasteless I was. Well, I was certainly tasteless enough to have married him, I'll give you that. Mind if I smoke?"

Don and I both shook our heads, though I think we both minded. But there was no point in cutting off a witness this forthcoming. Anyway, Don had told me that the bottle had not been recorked; they could tell, and a whole slew of people had seen someone uncork it at the party.

"What about Haycock's children?" Don said. "Of course, they've been investigated and interviewed, but I'd be grateful for your take on them."

" 'Take on them' is good. I wouldn't take them for all the tea in China, as my grandma used to say. Well, let me see. Hallam's not the oldest, but he acts as if he is; he's as horrible as his father but in a different way. Amazing, isn't it, how many ways men find of being horrible?" she said to me. "No insult intended," she added, looking at Don. "He was a stuffed shirt like his father, but more about money and against Democrats and feminists than to do with Tennyson or any other poet. I'm not a feminist, so I've never understood what they're going on about, but if Hallam hates them there must be something to be said on their side; the same for Democrats."

"And Charles Jr.?" Don said, to keep her off politics. I believe in letting witnesses run off at the mouth; you learn a lot that way. But I guess Don thought we'd be there all night if we didn't keep her on track.

"Chuck is the oldest, but he's smaller than Hallam,

and quieter than Hallam, and the only one of the three who seemed to think I had a right to be living, let alone with their father. I think he disliked Hallam and his father as much as I did, as much as I came to dislike them. I wasn't buddies with Chuck, but we got on all right."

"Did he live at home?" I asked. I thought Don probably knew the answer to that, but I wanted to keep her talking. I could sense that she was tiring a bit; quite often you need to get witnesses going again, before they've really run down.

"None of them lived at home. The daughter, Maud, was the closest to Daddy. I suppose girls often are. She was quite young when her mother died, and Daddy was a comfort, I suppose. She'd gotten married a short time ago, to a guy who traveled around the world a lot, India and places like that, so she came to see Daddy more often than I cared for; he liked it. If you want my opinion, the poor girl never had a chance, but I don't think she'd have killed Papa. She's the only one who I think is really sorry he's dead, if you'll excuse my bluntness. Hallam wants what there is to get, and he'd love to have me blamed for the death, but I think he's given up that hope. Chuck is relieved, is my guess, and Maud, like I said, is sorry."

"Ms. Burke," Don asked, consulting his notes, though that's just a thing you do to sound businesslike;

all police detectives do it. "Do you know if there were any members of the English department at the college with whom your husband had a close relationship— that is, someone who was a friend, or someone he particularly disliked?"

"Well, he certainly disliked that woman professor. Couldn't stand her. I think he spent a lot more time worrying about her than she did about him, but what do I know?"

I looked at Don to indicate I knew something about this, so there wasn't a need to pursue it, unless he especially wanted to. He didn't. "Were there any friends in the department, men he felt closely allied with?" Don asked.

"He would have said so, but I wouldn't have. They didn't all agree with him as chairman, and some of them wanted his job. He was really afraid that woman would get it, and one of the men said to him here, one night at dinner, that if she were chairman he would leave the department. I thought that guy was an arrogant fool and that the department would be better off without him, but I wouldn't want any woman as head of any place where I worked, so maybe he was right."

I would have liked to argue the point, but didn't; you never can. One speaks to witnesses for what they can tell you, and even if they turn out to be fascist pigs or into family values, you just let them get on with it. It's

not the easiest part of the job. I'd like to have asked her
if not wanting to obey a man in marriage was in any
way related to not wanting to obey a woman on the job,
but forget it. She wasn't the most thoughtful person,
this Ms. Burke, but then if she'd ever decided to marry
Haycock, she wasn't likely to do much thinking.

"So you don't believe that any of Professor Haycock's
three children could have wanted to kill him?" Don
asked. I guessed he was hoping that some more facts
about her and them and their relationship might arise if
she decided to be frank enough.

"Hallam is the likeliest, but I don't think he'd have
the guts. Besides, in his own peculiar way, I think Hallam liked the old fart—sorry," she added, smiling at
Don. That made me wonder if he wanted me to play
bad cop. I was on the alert for a signal. He nodded at
her to keep going.

"Chuck wouldn't kill his father or anyone; he's not
the sort." I wondered if she thought murderers all
looked the part, but didn't say so. "As for Maud, like I
said, she seemed to care for her father, but maybe that
was all an act and she really hated him. Although, now
that I think of it, it would have made more sense for her
to have murdered me."

"But all the children knew you didn't drink retsina?"
Don asked.

"Oh, God, they sure did. He made me taste it once; I

nearly threw up. If I want to drink Mr. Clean, I said, I've got some under the kitchen sink, thank you very much."

Don glanced my way for a second. "Still," I said, "it might have been clever of you to put it in that drink exactly because everyone knew you would never drink it."

"Everyone knew no one else would drink it. Not even lovey-dovey Maud could stomach the stuff. And if you think I'd wipe out the whole family without caring which one went first, well, all I can say is, you'll have to prove it. As for me, just getting the hell out of his house was all that was ever on my mind."

"Of course," I said, as Don stood up. "I didn't mean to suggest otherwise." I too got to my feet.

"Thank you, Ms. Burke," Don said. "You've been very good about answering our difficult questions."

"That's all right," she said. "I know you've got to clear this thing up. But," she added, looking at me, "I hope you don't think I would have killed him. To tell the truth, the idea never occurred to me."

"Of course it didn't," I said, and smiled at her, making up, as it were. I wasn't used to conducting an interview with someone else, and I hoped I hadn't been too rough on her.

We said our goodbyes, and walked silently out the building and down to Don's car.

"You were right to ask that last question," he said.

"The one that got her mad. Her response was spontaneous and told me what I wanted to know, which was that she'd never for a moment thought of dropping a deadly pill into the old guy's nasty drink."

"Did you ever suspect her?" I asked.

"Officially, I suspect everyone," he said as we drove off. "Personally, I don't think she did it; I never did think she did it. What I think now is that we have time for that dessert before your train."

CHAPTER EIGHT

And it was she who, while attending an "intellectual" dinner where everyone was supposed to give an opinion on adultery, said airily—and impertinently—"I'm so sorry, I prepared incest by mistake."
        —Edmund White, *Marcel Proust*

Naturally, or so it seemed to me, I wanted to call up Kate the next morning and request an afternoon meeting. I wanted to ask her who said, "she for the god in him," and I wanted to tell her what I had learned—not much—and what I'd figured out from what I'd learned: even less. But, I reminded myself, I was supposed to be doing my job, which was in New Jersey, not conferring with the likes of Kate Fansler, however much I wanted to do just that.

It did occur to me, as I stuffed my backpack with the necessities, now including a cell phone with which the ecstatic Octavia had presented me on my arrival, that I had had more stimulating conversations since the beginning of this job than in most of the rest of my detective career. I decided I had to protect myself against this new form of flirtation—well, new to me, anyway—and to ask some hard, pointed questions. My trouble was, I told myself after waving goodbye to Octavia, that I'd let my suspects set the agenda when talking to me. I'd learned about Virginia Woolf's play *Freshwater,* and about Dean Kimberly's gutsy decisions about her children, and about Antonia's views of the department, but only Kate Fansler, without sounding off, had actually explained something in direct answer to my questions, and Kate wasn't a suspect or even part of the scene of the crime. Pull yourself together, Woody, I ordered.

Riding out there, I went over the list of professors, all ranks, and reminded myself what they taught and what I knew about them. In most cases, damn little. I'd talked to David Longworth and Antonia Lansbury; Haycock was dead, but I'd talked to his wife recently, and his children before the anonymous letter had widened the field of departmental suspects.

I also knew all there was to know about digoxin that could be gathered anywhere. It was a certain cause of death, and seemed to be a bit too readily available for so toxic a drug, but then, I had to remind myself, most folks weren't trying to kill themselves or anybody else. It's widely prescribed for anyone with a history of atrial fibrillation, which is, I had learned, the most common cardiac dysrhythmia. Haycock, who had cardiac dysrhythmia along with all his personality defects, kept a supply. So do many other people. The family, wife and children, used to get Haycock's prescription refilled for him—they were known to the pharmacist he used—but it wasn't clear at the time and probably never would be whether the digoxin used was from Haycock's supply or someone else's.

Don had told me the police were looking into that; it was so common a drug, however, and easy enough to make from the even more common foxglove plant, that the source was unlikely to offer much of a clue to the person who'd dropped eight 250-microgram pills into Haycock's retsina. Given that he had heart trouble, fewer would also have worked, suggesting that we didn't have a specialist in heart medicine among our suspects, but then we knew that already. Anyhow, information about digoxin was easily gotten—look how much of it I knew by heart, when I couldn't remember why a play of Virginia Woolf's should have annoyed the chief victim. No wonder Kate was in demand for literary-type murders; you had to be one to know one, as the saying goes.

When I swung off the highway and onto the smaller road leading to the college, I went over in my mind who exactly I was going to meet up with today, even if I had to pursue them to their homes. I have a trained memory, which, so far at least, has always produced what previously acquired information I asked of it, but I don't burden it unnecessarily: last names only for Clifton's English department, except for Antonia and

Dawn. So I had to track down Goldberg, American Literature; Petrillo, Medieval; Wanamaker, Comparative; Janeer, Romantic, not tenured; Lermann, Eighteenth Century, tenured but only an assistant prof; then there was Graham, Novel, untenured, and Oakwood, Creative Writing, adjunct. Thank God one of the cast of characters was on leave. This could take all day. Well, it *would* take all day, but I was ready.

Dawn had told me that Tuesdays, Wednesdays, and Thursdays were the best days to find everyone around. Fridays many of them took off if there wasn't an important meeting, and Monday they were still a little spacey—my word, not hers—from the weekend. These professor types seemed not only to be the most disagreeable bunch I'd ever heard of outside of the criminal world, but they were also the luckiest. Maybe it wouldn't be bad to sit at home reading Tennyson and writing about him, and then holding forth on him in the classroom. Maybe there was something I was missing here, but it did seem as though hating each other provided the only real excitement available.

Dawn was busy when I came, but she greeted me and handed me a schedule that showed who would be in their office, a classroom, or home at what hour. Very useful. I had all their résumés, of course—CVs, they called them. The department had started to protest when I asked for those, but I said, "Either help me or find yourself another private eye." I meant it too. Truth is, I wouldn't have known to ask for the damn things, but the police had found them after arming themselves with a search warrant—Haycock had wanted to be chairman, after all; they needed to look around his office—and Don had told me about them.

I decided to begin with Petrillo, Medieval, who was having office hours even as I arrived and who sounded the nicest of the men. Petrillo had published a lot, most of it about people I'd never heard of, unlike Tennyson and Shakespeare and Virginia Woolf, and half of whom seemed not to have written in English—but the number of student committees Petrillo had served on, and the fact that he was teaching a course on race in addition to his regular schedule and his regular period, made me think he might be more human than the others.

I waited outside his office door for the last student to depart, then introduced myself. Petrillo got to his feet and welcomed me as though I were someone he was really glad to see. Watch it, Woody, I said to myself. Don't get bamboozled again by a charming intellectual who knows how to manipulate conversation. Even Longworth, after all, had told me exactly what he wanted me to know, and had done it charmingly.

"Ask away," Petrillo said, leaving me to set the tone. I asked all the necessaries. Yes, he was at Haycock's house that day and stayed around for quite a while, being a convivial type, which was far from easy here—waving his arm to indicate the department's territory. Yes, he saw Haycock die, or anyway collapse. It was he, Petrillo, who had dialed for help, and he'd already told some nice policeman whom he'd seen there. Did I want him to repeat it?

I had a real talker here, I could see that. I asked how he felt about Haycock.

"Not a nice person," Petrillo said, "but an honest one. The trouble with most of the right-wing boys, frankly, is that they lie so easily there's no reason to believe anything they say. Haycock's ideas were crazy, and he was certainly a bit feudal about Tennyson—no trespassing, no reason for anybody else to be there—but you knew how he felt and where he stood. He considered women an inferior species, designed to serve man, not to equal him or, heaven forbid, to try to rule with him, but at least he said what he thought. Believe me, around here that's almost admirable, even if his opinions were antediluvian even in Tennyson's time."

" 'He for God, she for the god in him,' " I said.

Petrillo didn't even look surprised at a private eye's quoting that. I paused a minute, hoping he'd mention the author, but he didn't. Well, he'd assume I knew what I was talking about, wouldn't he?

"So, hypothetically speaking," I said, "even if you'd had the chance to murder someone in this department and get away with it, you wouldn't have picked Haycock?"

"That's a terrible question for an officer of the law to ask," he said, quite shocked. "You are an officer of the law, aren't you? Well, whether you are or not, surely you can't suppose that any sane person would want to murder anyone, especially someone he knew?"

"You'd be surprised," I said. "But I do apologize if I've offended you. Not that many people believe in sin these days, and murder's only the biggest sin of all."

"There are probably worse sins," he said. "I'm a Catholic and I believe in sin; not everybody does. I don't say the Church and the pope are not responsible for serious crimes, but that has nothing to do with my beliefs."

"I guess you have to explain that to a lot of people," I said.

"Yes, I do. But I shouldn't be preaching to you. What else can I tell you?"

"Well, frankly, this department seems a pretty unpleasant place. Everybody seems suspicious of everybody else, and half of them are frightened of something or other. Why do you think that is?"

"Why do *I* think it is, or why is it? Or are those the same question?"

"Most people think they are."

"Too true. As to why is it, it's never easy for those who have long languished in unchallenged power, power awarded them because of their sex, their color, and their family background, to tolerate, much less welcome, insurgents who are challenging their domain. No one is going to give up the old privileges of being an important professor or an old-fashioned husband or the teacher of canonical texts—not easily, not readily, not without a good deal of force being applied. Why should they? A few odd, quirky types like me want to do the right thing, but we're usually called fools and worse for feeling that way. Mostly, if people out of power want to have a share in that power or even take it away altogether from those who've always had it—that is a revolution. Even in my long-ago period, the smart chaps knew that if you give the underdog the smallest bit of power, he—or she—is going to want more and more. That's how it is."

I nodded; nothing new here, though I must say I couldn't get over marveling at the way these people talked.

"Why do *I* think it's worse here?" he continued, not missing a beat. "Because we have not, alas, collected a bunch of good people, differing in their views, perhaps, but basically broad-minded and generous. No, indeed. And that's not an accident," he added, sensing what I was about to ask. These guys not only talk more and with longer words, they answer questions before they're asked. I suppose it comes from teaching.

"Those in power," he said, "tend to attract to them, and to attach to them, others like them. They want colleagues who agree with them, who think the same remarks are funny and the same jokes allowable. That explains this department, I'm afraid."

"How did they happen to attract you?" I couldn't help asking.

"Well, medievalists are rather different. It isn't easy to tell from their writings or their shop talk how they feel about contemporary life—not right off the bat, anyway. I wanted this job. My wife works in New Jersey—she's a surgeon, in a good place for a woman surgeon, comparatively speaking—so I guess I didn't go out of my way to say disturbing or aggressive things."

Well, Woody, I thought, if he's leading you astray, he's damn good at it. I'd have to see if this struck Kate the way it struck me. I had to admit once again that Claire Wiseman sure knew what she was doing when she told me I needed someone to consult re academia.

"Just one more question," I said. "If you had to pick the likeliest among your colleagues to have dropped the pill in Haycock's Greek drink, who would that be? Please be frank; I won't tell anyone, but I do need help here." I'd gathered, of course, that he was the sort who would always want to help if he could.

"I don't mind the question," he said, "but I can't answer it. I've thought about it a good deal: who among them would be willing to have murder on his soul? Oddly enough—perhaps because none of them is Catholic, or not so's you'd notice—I thought that any one of them could have done it, or couldn't possibly have done it, depending on how you looked at it at any one time. I know that's not much help, but there it is, I'm afraid."

"Thank you for your honesty," I said, getting up and grabbing my bag and helmet.

"A pleasure," he said, rising also. "Not the subject, alas, but talking with you. I've never before met a private detective. I'm glad we hired you." So he was helping to pay my fee also. One thing I didn't know, and would probably never know, was who had willingly kicked in to the agreement to hire and pay me, and who had been dragged in because of what not taking part might suggest.

Wanamaker, Comparative, turned out to have taken his students to some exhibit somewhere, and would have to be postponed. Goldberg, American, was lecturing; I decided to drop in and listen to him. At least I could get some impression, and not waste time getting it one-on-one. It was a crazy case, really. They could all have done it; they all had motives, at least one as good as the other; and the only ones with the biggest motives were the ones I didn't want to have done it. Not a very professional attitude, but there you are.

Goldberg glanced up when I came into the lecture hall through a squeaky door at the back, but he didn't take much notice of me. I slid into a chair next to a guy who seemed to be sleeping; his feet were on the seat in front of him, and his chair was tilted back against the wall. He straightened it up when I came in and stared at me. The helmet seemed to win his attention. I smiled at him—it always pays to seem friendly—and turned my attention to Goldberg. He was holding forth about the American tradition, with a lot about God and puritanism and veils; at least, I thought he said veils, the sort that cover a woman's face; I got that much. But there wasn't much more to get, in my opinion, unless you were into guilt and stuff. The guy next to me seemed to agree; he took a piece of paper from his notebook, which I gathered he carried as a form of disguise, since there was nothing in it, and scribbled a note to me: *What kind of bike?* it said.

Yamaha, I scribbled back. *What book is he talking about?* I added, nodding at the professor as I handed the paper back.

Who the fuck knows? he wrote in return, handing me the paper with an enormous shrug of his shoulders. I had kept my eye on Goldberg, who frowned in our direction; I tried to look apologetic and humble. But he wasn't glaring at me; he was glaring at my dozing, note-passing companion. "Mr. Ferguson," Goldberg said, spitting out every syllable, "I have no objection to your sleeping; I quite understand that my taking attendance persuades you to sleep here rather than elsewhere. I would, however, appreciate your not conversing, vocally or by pen, with anyone else."

Mr. Ferguson saluted in answer, tipped his chair back, and closed his eyes. I thought his behavior unnecessarily rude, but Goldberg certainly seemed to be a pompous ass, and not exactly courtesy himself.

When the lecture was over, Mr. Ferguson exited with haste, but he waited for me on the stairs. "Could I see it?" he asked. "Your wheels?" he added as I looked bewildered.

"It's over in the parking lot," I said. "I think it's the only bike there. You can look, but don't lay a finger on it; I'll know where to look if there's so much as a fingerprint."

"Got you," he said.

We continued down the stairs together. "Mr. Ferguson," I said. "You don't seem to care much for American literature. Why are you in the class?"

"You have to take a certain amount of lit beyond the survey. I had Petrillo for the survey; an okay guy, but he tended to stick around old times. I mean, who cared what they were doing that long ago? I thought American lit would at least make some sense, but forget it. Goldberg is not only a shit, he's a boring shit. Like calling me Mr. Ferguson. He calls all the others he bothers to notice, or who bother to suck up to him, by their first names. I'm not worthy of that honor."

"I wonder," I began, and then decided not to beat around the bush. "Why are you in college at all if it bores you out of your mind?"

"Sports," he said, as though that explained everything. I looked my question.

"Yeah, sports at Clifton, if you can believe it. I hardly can. They play in some league so minor no one's ever heard of any of the colleges. But hell, they gave me a scholarship, and the folks thought it would do me good to go to college and help me to get on in the world. Not all the courses are that bad; he's the dullest and the biggest prick. None of them's great either."

"Do many students feel the way you do?" I asked. "About Goldberg and the college in general?"

"Many do; they have these stupid required courses— an asshole idea. There's too much lit required, and most of the students think these old guys are like from some other universe. Well, nice talking with you; I'm off to look at your bike and feel it up a little. Just kidding. Don't freak."

Somehow there didn't seem much point in waiting around to talk to Goldberg. I didn't mind Petrillo mentioning sin, but there's only so much religious stuff I can stand in one day. I went back to the department and waited outside some more office doors. I didn't learn much. If one of these professors was hiding a murderous hatred, or an act of murder, he or she was not going to let it all hang out during their first interview with me.

My last encounter that day was with Kevin Oakwood, the adjunct teacher of creative writing. When I got to his office and explained who I was and what I wanted, he told me he couldn't sit still another minute, and if I wanted his perspective, I'd have to buy him a drink. I agreed, and off we went, he with a briefcase stuffed with papers and I with my bag and helmet. He didn't question the helmet. I got the impression other people didn't interest him much, least of all fat, no-longer-really-young women. He marched at a great pace and I followed like a pet bulldog.

He led the way to a seedy bar, hardly devoid of students but unlikely, I gathered, to appeal to students who might want to corner him and talk about their writing. He did, however, accept several greetings in a way that suggested he was not above picking up companionship here, and would probably do so when I had left. It didn't take a detective to figure that out.

We sat at a small table. I offered to go to the bar and

get the drinks, which seemed the right thing to do. It also avoided his asking me what I wanted, which was nothing alcoholic; if I got it myself, the seltzer might look like gin and tonic. He wanted beer, a large one. "The thirst those creative types create is unbelievable," he told me.

When I returned with his beer and my drink, which he didn't even glance at, he gulped beer for a while, and then lit a cigarette. "I guess you must be the detective they've hired about the murder of Lord Tennyson," he said. "Yes, I was there that day, and no, I didn't do it. What else can I tell you?"

"I'm surprised you teach creative writing if you don't like the students or their work," I said, hoping to get a rise out of him. A lot of useful stuff rises with rises.

"Jesus, sweetie, where did they dig you up? I know there're some writers who like teaching writing, encouraging the young and all that, but mostly they're poets and mostly they're ladies, and mostly they couldn't write themselves out of a wet paper bag. I write novels, and I teach writing to pay the rent and buy the necessaries. Like beer," he said, finishing his off.

"Have another," I said, figuring that was the only way to keep him there any longer.

"Thanks, I think I will," he said. I got up to get it for him. I could have made him get it, but I needed to pay for it, and the thought of handing him the money didn't sit well. I suspected he wouldn't bring back any change.

He started talking as soon as I was back. "The real trouble," he said, "isn't the students; they're not bad, they like to write about kinky sex and quirky parents—well, I guess I encourage that, but I have to read the damn stuff, don't I? It's the older women, the alumnae, who are allowed to take the course. They've all decided to write their stories, and believe me, their stories are as exciting as their bodies, which is to say not at all. I mean, who the fuck cares about their marriages or their affairs or their bloody children? And I can't tell them to go home and do some laundry, because if I make them happy they may give the college a little token of thanks for the college kitty and say it was all due to me. It's to puke."

"You are a member of the English department?" I said, putting it as a question.

"Hardly a member. Just under their rule, and they pay my meager salary. I don't go to meetings and I don't know anybody in the fucking department, so it's no good interrogating me."

"But you went to Haycock's party."

"Got an invitation, which is to say a command. No good insulting the guy. I didn't stay long, though. Of course, I didn't know someone would bump him off after I left, or I might have hung around for the big event."

"It wasn't worth staying for the free drinks?"

"Hardly. I'd already packed away a few. And one of the students hired to pass around the drinks and nibbly bits slipped me a large Scotch, so I was feeling just about right when I left."

"Is she in your writing class?"

"Was. I give her more private lessons now. Well, you know," he added, as though it had occurred to him that perhaps he wasn't making a terribly good impression, "she's here on a scholarship and has to work besides. I bring a little bit of frivolity into her demanding life."

"Would you care to guess at who, of those you know in the department, might have wanted to kill Professor Haycock?"

"Anyone with all his or her marbles. The guy was crackers, and had far too much power. He even suggested that I get the students in my classes to write Tennysonian verse. I told him I don't teach poetry, but what I would have liked to tell him was . . . Well, he was paying my pittance, wasn't he? Or the department was, and he could have stopped it. I can't be sure the next chairman will even want a creative writing program, so why kill off the old fool I was sure of? That suit you for an answer? As to who else would want to knock him off, I haven't a clue."

"Thank you," I said. "You've been very helpful. I appreciate your giving me the time."

"Hey, no rush, is there? Don't you want another G and T?"

"One's enough for me," I said, and walked away. But as I was leaving, I saw him move over toward one of the girl students. Well, I thought as I trudged back to the parking lot, if someone murdered him I wouldn't even take the case.

CHAPTER NINE

We, we have chosen our path—
Path to a clear-proposed goal,
Path of Advance!
  —Matthew Arnold, "Rugby Chapel"

The next evening I sat in Kate's living room spilling
my guts. I was feeling humiliated, insecure, and in need
of consolation and support. I would really have liked to
lie down on the floor next to Banny and rest my head on
her huge body, but I sat up in a chair and, fortified by
the drink Kate had offered, tried to display what dignity I could muster. It wasn't much. Kate listened sym-
pathetically and didn't try to interrupt or halt my
complaint; she allowed it all to spill out.

"I'm out of my depth, useless, incompetent, and in-
adequate," I announced, just for starters. "I'm a pretty
efficient person, or thought I was. I get results; I have a
good record; most of my cases are satisfactorily concluded. I size people up, figure them out, catch all the
nuances, especially the unintended ones; I'm a good listener, and until this horrible case came along, I would
have told you I was a good detective—first-rate, in fact.
On this bloody assignment, I find myself spinning

around in a state of bewilderment. I don't know what to make of what anybody says, except maybe the Haycock family. That's familiar enough.

"But I ask you: plays about Tennyson and required courses and tenure decisions and Freud worship—give me a break. I'm resigning, in fact. I thought it only right to tell you first. Next comes Claire Wiseman, then Don Jackson. Then I write a formal admission of failure to the family and the English department at that lousy college, together with a bill for the time I spent. After all, I did work for them, and success is not guaranteed, although in my own mind I always thought it was."

Kate opened her mouth to speak, but I beat her to the punch. "Don't try to talk me out of quitting. I went to college, I went to law school—it isn't as though I'd never had an academic experience. I might as well have been running this investigation in a small foreign country with an unknown language. I don't wonder people came to you to investigate their academic crimes. Who else could possibly get what the people in today's crazy institutions of higher learning were talking about."

I stopped because I was practically out of breath, and anyway I couldn't think of any more angry statements. Maybe I put it on a bit thick, but everything I said was true. I hated letting Kate down, and Don, but for the rest—well, it was my first absolute failure and I hoped never to think about any of it ever again. Also, I should in honesty add that since I'd come in the evening, leaving my bike at home, I'd enjoyed my drink and was set to go on to more if asked. Kate had said she had more time in the evening, and today I was going to need it; perhaps she had figured that out.

"Surely," Kate said, "there have been cases that seemed unintelligible at some point, where you thought you'd better just bow out. I've never worked on a problem where I didn't feel like that at least once in a major way—more often in a minor way. I expect you're really farther along than you know. I think you need to talk it through. I'm listening."

I accepted another drink, single malt Scotch—it goes down smooth and doesn't seem to cause the usual confusion in one's mental capacities; they just loosen up a bit. The drinks certainly didn't stop me from giving Kate a neat account of the bloody affair, not quite from the beginning—she'd heard that—but from the last time we'd met. I had to backtrack just a little to fill in now and then, but on the whole I did well. Kate thought so too.

I'd come provided with a list; she already had the department list and the family list, but I added the names of everyone who had set foot in the Haycock house on the day he keeled over. Everyone, down to delivery men, student helpers, and Haycock relatives not earlier designated. Then I told her, word for word, every conversation I'd had. I described every place I'd been, I left out my interpretations or impressions, if any, but I accounted for every minute spent on the case. So by the time I wound down, Kate had all I had. Which wasn't much, or wasn't what I'd call coherent.

I shut up, took a sip of my drink, and looked expectant.

"This may sound wild," Kate said, "but I have to ask it. Can you be absolutely certain that Haycock didn't take the pills himself, that he didn't put them in his special wine and hope that someone else, anyone else, would be accused of murder? I know it's unlikely, but not unprecedented. Let's say he was simultaneously discouraged about the reception of his life's work on Tennyson, fed up with his family, and finding purpose and excitement in the thought of the havoc his death would cause. Is there any evidence that is not the case?"

"I can't say it's altogether impossible," I said, pulling myself together. "I did float the idea here and there, not to the family but to his colleagues. They all dismissed it as out of the question. The general opinion seemed to be that he was far too narcissistic to consider doing away with himself, even for the chance to cause general misery. Uppermost in his mind would be the thought that he wouldn't be there to see the fun. I also played around with the idea with Don Jackson; he'd thought of it too. If we don't find who did it, we may be able to console ourselves with this theory, however."

I took another sip, slowly. "I'd like to cling to your idea for dear life. But there's something else against it having been suicide. There was the same amount of digoxin in both the bottle of retsina and in Haycock's glass. If he could have put it in the glass to kill himself, why put it in the bottle too?"

"Am I missing something?" Kate asked. "If there was a certain amount of digoxin in the bottle and he had poured himself a glass, wouldn't you expect the two solutions to be the same?"

"You would, if he had put his self-administered dose in the bottle. But why do that? Why take the chance of someone else showing up who liked retsina, unlikely as that might be? Why not put his dose in his glass? Then he's safely dead and no one else is. If you see what I mean." It seemed to make sense to me, but perhaps the single malt Scotch was having more effect than I realized.

"I see what you mean. Neat deduction. But can we be sure Haycock, if he had decided to leave this world, would not want to take a few people with him? That might strike him as a suitable ending to the lack of appreciation he'd been dealt."

"Well, we can't have it both ways."

Kate nodded. "Good. Let's abandon that idea for now. I thought it important to mention. The other reflection that has occurred to me has to do with Tennyson. I mean, there has been a tendency on everyone's part—his colleagues first of all and then yours and mine—to consider his relative lunacy about Tennyson as particularly germane to his murder. But I tend to think that Tennyson was a symptom, not the cause."

"Antonia said that—that if Tennyson were the main motive, Haycock was likelier to have killed her. And what do you mean by *relative* lunacy?"

"Believe it or not, I've known cases of greater lunacy, of really mad devotion to one's subject. We all tend to get our own subjects a bit out of proportion; we defend those we have written about and resent others who cast aspersions, even reasonable ones. Then there are the real nuts like the Freudian advocates, who won't brook the slightest criticism or reinterpretation of holy writ. This type comes with devotion to a whole range of individual writers and thinkers. I'm not sure that Haycock quite reached the maniac dimension," Kate said, sighing. "But I think it was good to mention that, as well as the theory about suicide. They've cleared our heads a bit."

"They may have cleared your head," I said, "but they haven't done much for mine. The point, you see, is that I feel that I've wandered, or allowed myself to be led, into a situation beyond my capabilities. I've studied all the information I've gathered so far, I've looked at it upside down and backward, and it's . . . well, what I said—I don't really know this foreign country's culture or its language. I think the best thing for me to do would be to bow out. It would also be the fairest all around." I had the feeling that I might have said this before, but if so, I thought it would bear repeating.

In fact, I really felt awful, which is why the Scotch didn't seem to be making me drunk, or merry, or full of hope and resolution. I've noticed that there are times when one hopes for release by way of drink, and if the problem or fright is sufficiently serious, release does not come, as it had not come now.

I thought Kate might feel impatient, but she didn't. I suppose over the years she had dealt with enough discouraged students wrestling with their dissertations and convinced they'd picked the wrong subject to know what I was talking about. I decided to point this out.

"Look, surely you've had students who started writing on some literary subject, say Tennyson, and then they discovered, partway through, maybe halfway through, that they were so bored or annoyed by him and his poems that they couldn't continue. Well, that's how it is with me. Hasn't that happened?"

"Rarely, in fact," Kate said. "No, I'm not tampering with the truth in order to persuade you to continue. There have been one or two who quit, but not many. One I can think of was writing on Swinburne and had reached the point of total abhorrence. He said it was like that drug alcoholics take to stop drinking: any alcohol at all and they vomit. One more glance at a Swinburne poem and . . . well, you get the point. But most of the time, the writer of the dissertation needs to approach the subject from a different angle—often only slightly different, as it turns out—or needs to expand or contract the extent of the original idea. That happens quite often. Anyone who writes, let alone works on a dissertation, often has to switch gears, change the emphasis, cut the material to be covered, or move whole sections around. It doesn't mean that quitting is the only solution, and it seldom is the one taken."

"That's a nice little speech, and neatly applicable to my situation. Except that this job isn't a do-or-die situation; I just go on to other jobs more suited to my talents."

"Sorry if I sounded patronizing," Kate said. "I was just recalling the dissertations I'd sponsored and how they turned out. But I guess I was talking with a motive, which was to persuade you not to quit. You may not find the murderer; if you do find him or her, you may not be able to prove it. But for your own satisfaction, I don't think quitting is called for. Not yet."

I sighed. Deeply.

Kate laughed. "Look, Woody, if you really want to quit, you should. Don't worry about what I'll think, which will be nothing critical of you. Don't worry about what the people who hired you will think. Who knows what their motives are anyway? Just ask yourself how you'll feel after the satisfaction of signing off has started to dilute just a little."

"You sound convincing. You're ready to talk about the case with me, and I'm mighty grateful for that. Why do I get the feeling that you're keeping something back—that you don't want me to quit for all the reasons you've so movingly laid out, but that there's some other reason too? Maybe my suspecting this is just an indication that my intuition, when applied to academic, intellectual types and folks practiced in literary criticism, is out to lunch?"

Kate got up to get another drink. Once she was back in her seat, drink in hand, Banny moved over to her, thrusting her nose against her arm.

"She's telling me it's time to go out," Kate said, setting down her drink. "And it is. How about that walk we talked about the three of us taking?"

"At night, in the park, in the dark?" I asked. I'm used to danger, but I don't cultivate it in parks in the middle of the night—well, evening.

"I rather think that Banny, you, and I will be quite safe enough. Banny and I don't go into the park at night alone. Usually Reed is with us. It's become a routine, at least when possible. You'd be surprised how many people are in the park, and not all muggers and worse."

"It's a deal," I said. Probably the air would do me good. Also, I figured, if Kate was going to deliver a low blow, I'd rather be walking in the dark when it hit.

So the three of us strolled in the park, Banny ahead without a leash. "I thought big dogs had to be leashed now," I said. "One of the mayor's ways of interfering in city life."

"Not after nine at night," Kate said. "Or before nine in the morning. That is not an hour when I am conscious, but sometimes Reed takes her out then, if he's woken up early. Let's look at the lake. I always hope to see the swans. They mate for life, and arrive in pairs."

I kept quiet. We walked past the lake while Kate was pulling her thoughts together, deciding what to say, and how to say it.

She finally spoke. "Woody, what I'm going to say is just a suspicion, a theory, no more likely to be true than my earlier idea about Haycock's possible suicide. What I'm going to say isn't necessarily the truth, has no foundation other than supposition, and may be nonsense."

I nodded, though I didn't know if she could see me nod. "Go on," I said. "Tell me your second wild idea."

"You see, you remember that earlier I said I had a wild idea. You remember words; you're smart. I've learned how smart you are. But as you say, this isn't the sort of case you usually undertake or, in fact, have ever undertaken. Also, you tend to make remarks about your being fat, which also makes a certain impression. What I'm trying to say is—"

"I get it," I said, interrupting her rather loudly. "I get it. You think they hired me because I was too stupid to figure it out, because they knew that with me on the trail, the murderer would get away with it. They hoped I'd be just as bamboozled as . . . as I am, in fact. That was the whole idea. Is that what you were going to tell me?"

"That's it, Woody. But that's not all of it. I think Claire Wiseman guessed at that motive for hiring you, or suspected it. But because she knew a bit more about you than the Clifton people did, because you'd done a good job with her friend, she decided to, well, urge you to get me on board."

"Kate," I shouted. "I can't believe you used a phrase like *on board*. Did telling me this make you as nervous as all that?"

"You're damn right," Kate said. "The way I figure it, assuming the truth of my premises, Claire decided that if she was right I might protect you from becoming unduly discouraged; if she was wrong, well, nothing would have been lost by our brainstorming together from time to time on your case."

"Brainstorming," I shouted. "That's almost as bad as *on board.*"

"Reed has pointed out to me that I tend to fall into clichés when under emotional stress. It's a sign he has long since learned to read. Now you can read it too." And she took a small plastic bag from her pocket and bent down to retrieve Banny's poop. She dropped the bag into a trash can as we walked by.

"In London," she said, "they have separate receptacles for dog refuse, as they call it. A damn good idea, but the English are more orderly than Americans."

"Okay," I said, ignoring this. "I'm not quitting. I'm going over it all again, with you, with Don, and in my head. And they can all take their academic arrogance and shove it. Can't Banny walk any faster than that?"

CHAPTER TEN

The world will not believe a man repents;
And this wise world of ours is mainly right.
　　　　　　—Tennyson, *Idylls of the King*

The next day was again New Jersey, but I went this time as a transformed woman: I was feeling my oats, much friskier and more determined in my mind; I wasn't about to be humbled again by academics. I had called Antonia Lansbury that morning and told her that I needed a long session with her and needed it soon. She said that today was her day without classes, could I come to her house, and what time would I be there. I said one o'clock, and arranged to meet Don Jackson beforehand. It's amazing what powers one can call upon when told those very powers have been underestimated. *Very* underestimated, as I hoped to demonstrate. Well, I knew I might fail, but I was certainly going to try.

I went on my bike this time. Neither drinking nor late socializing was in the program, and I wanted to be able to get around on my own. Don was nice about offering rides, but independence is important. Besides, I might be able to give him another lift. I'd discovered that once I got over my anxieties about his sitting in back of me, I rather liked it.

We met at the diner—I thought of it as "our place," as in "our song"; I'm a great one for instant tradition, which I prefer to the long-lasting kind. I had breakfast, and he had lunch. I would eat breakfast for every meal if there were someone to fix it for me; nothing is better than breakfast.

I told him I was going to see Antonia; I told him I felt they'd jerked us around long enough, and that I intended to ask some hard questions and get some answers—or determine what the avoidance of answers meant. I asked him if the police had done much of a check on the kids from the college who had come to serve and bartend at the Haycock affair. He said he had their names and records.

"Tell me about them," I said. "I just hadn't known they were there."

"Scholarship kids and kids who need to earn money register with the employment office, which sends them out for parties, baby-sitting, lawn mowing, general kinds of help. A lot of people in the town use them. Faculty and administrators who give parties, as well as people in the town, hire them. It's the usual thing. There were three of them at the Haycock party—one serving food, one in the kitchen, one tending bar. It's the standard arrangement. All those who get work through the office are vetted, and records are kept of where they work, and complaints if any."

"Do people ever request certain students back again?"

"Quite often, I gather, but that wasn't the case with Haycock. He just called in—his wife being away—and left a general order for three helpers."

"Just trying to fill in the blank spaces," I said. "Ever hopeful, that's me."

"What are you planning to ask Antonia?"

"A lot more details about life in Clifton's English department and maybe elsewhere. If I learn anything, you'll be the first to hear. I got a cell phone, by the way; here's the number." Octavia had had new cards printed up with my cell phone number on them, and I handed him one. I had objected that with these cards anyone could call me on the cell phone instead of at the office, which was far preferable. Among other advantages she, Octavia, could answer. She told me to keep both sets of cards, and only give the one with the cell phone number on it to those who might need to reach me in a hurry. The trouble with having an efficient assistant is that one stops thinking for oneself on practical matters. Well, Octavia was worth it.

"Do you often have unsolved murders?" I asked Don.

"We don't often have murders," he said. "Not like this. At the worst, hit-and-run drivers or husbands who batter their wives and children or the occasional robbery or mugging or fight that ends badly. There's not much scope for detectives around here, and the police aren't too eager to get in too deep with the college. There's some resentment of it because it doesn't pay taxes, and some recognition that the college brings in a lot more money than would be here without it. One of the reasons I'm glad that they hired a private eye—you—is that you can come in, do your work, and leave. We have to hang around when all the shouting dies down."

"But no one on the police force thinks I'm going to get anywhere. I know—don't bother to contradict me. The point is, I'll fail but all the right moves will have been made. The college and the police who cooperated with me can say they really tried to do the right thing."

"There's probably some truth in that," Don said. "Personally, I hope you'll solve this thing, and I mean to help you if I can. I'm telling you more than my captain thinks I am, so you might say we're in this together, in a manner of speaking. You'll get the credit or the blame, no doubt of that, depending on how it comes out. I'm betting that you come through, but I wouldn't count on any tokens of appreciation if I were you. This seems to be one murder no one wants solved, except maybe the family, and they want the killer found only if it's the wife."

"Thanks for your frankness," I said. "Anywhere I can drop you?"

"I hoped you'd ask; I walked here." We paid and left; we each paid for our own food and left our own tip. Don said it seemed better, if we were going to go on meeting this way, and I hoped we were.

He slid behind me onto the bike as though we did this every day. I wish. When I dropped him off he said, "How about giving me a call on that new cell phone when you finish with the lady professor? You can tell me how it went."

"You're on," I said, "but don't call her a lady professor; just like I'm not a lady detective. Plain *professor* and *detective* will do nicely."

"Got it," Don said.

Antonia lived in a large house, the way everyone did around here; it was a very big house with a lot of land around it. She said the college had, through some mortgage arrangements, made it possible for her to buy it, as they did for all the faculty, hoping they'd stay near the college and not commute. She told me this as she beckoned me in the door, down the hall, and into her study.

"It's the only room where I can shut a door with some assurance that I won't be disturbed. The rest of the house is family territory. My husband, who's a doctor, also has a study, but it seems to be more of a place where he and the children hang out. Any papers or computers connected to his work are in his office."

I liked her study, and I could understand why she didn't use her office to work in. This room was where she belonged; anyone could see that. "How many children?" I asked, just to get started.

"Two," she said. "Teenagers."

"Is it as awful as they say, living with teenagers?" It wasn't a warm-up question; I really wondered.

"Yes and no," she said. "Yes, because they have to break away and act as though their parents couldn't and didn't have the right slant on anything. No, because we had so frantically girded our loins in anticipation of nameless horrors that the actual experience seems mild by comparison—at least for the present. But how can I help you?"

We both sat on chairs. She'd removed papers from one of them—visitors weren't expected in this place. She probably was used to sitting in the other chair herself, which explained its availability.

I settled back as though I intended to stay for a long interview, my notebook at the ready. I was trying to adopt an introductory pose. In fact, an introduction was what I couldn't really think of so I decided to plunge right in.

"Professor Lansbury," I began.

She waved and said, "Antonia, please. And you're Woody."

"Antonia," I began again, "as far as I can make out from what I've learned and what I've picked up in various conversations, you appear to be at the heart of, well, the department's ill nature. I don't for a minute mean," I hastened to say as she looked ready to object, "that it's your fault. Quite the contrary, I'd say. It's just that, when I try to figure out why your name always comes up when someone sympathetic to you mentions the lack of harmony—"

" 'Lack of harmony' puts it sweetly but hardly describes the rank unpleasantness and resentment we all exist in. And yes, I can see why you think I'm the focus of all this. Because, in a way, I am. Through no fault of my own, as you say, except for being who I am, where I am, and at this time."

I nodded encouragingly.

"Did you happen to see an article in the *New York Times* not long ago? I have it here somewhere," she said, looking around as though she might be able to spot it from where she sat. "It was headlined: 'M.I.T. Acknowledges Bias against Female Professors.' The president of M.I.T. is quoted saying that he had always supposed that discrimination against women, while existing, was largely a matter of perception. He now admits that it is a matter of reality. The report, which got so much publicity because it comes from a university famous for its science, and because the report was based on data, nonetheless recognizes that women are constantly being slighted, ignored, and blocked for promotion, grants, and important university work."

"What sort of data?" I asked. I really wondered how you could count facts in matters like this.

"The data had to do with evidence that women are not often hired, and that when they get tenure they are increasingly marginalized by the male-dominated networks. But the report also mentioned smaller slights, less easily converted to data, such as—and any established woman professor can testify to this—that when a woman suggests something at a meeting she is unheard; later, when a man suggests the same thing, the suggestion is seriously taken up. And so on. The odd part about women's problems in academia is that the higher you rise, the more the male networks and individuals fear you, and the more marginalized and hated you become. This isn't universal, but it's prevalent. Does that answer your question?"

"You're saying that because you are a tenured professor, you are treated badly and feared."

"That's putting it baldly, but it's not too exaggerated

at the moment. The whole atmosphere in our department, as I've said, became really poisonous when an assistant professor, highly qualified and teaching modern literature, came up for tenure. She deserved it by every possible criterion, but full of fear of her subject; of her work, which might include gendered interpretations of literature about which they felt defensive; of her popularity with the students; and, perhaps most of all, of her friendship with me and our mutual support—well, they contrived to deny her tenure. The administration, little different from our department and close friends with many of them, went along. They had to do a good bit of nasty, dishonest work to keep her out. They know the department is too heavily male, but they fear change. The upshot was that things were not rosy before Catherine came up for tenure, but they've been hideous since."

I sat back to absorb this. Antonia realized she had become, not excited, but certainly less calm than she would have liked, and she looked to me as though she was about to make excuses. So I spoke.

"Rick Fowler told me that there had been some huge ruckus about a play by Virginia Woolf that you wanted to put on, a play that Haycock decided was insulting to him and, I suppose, Tennyson."

Antonia leaned back and laughed. Her chair was one

of those that tips over backward, and I expected her to struggle against falling, but apparently she was used to it. " 'She is coming, my dove, my dear,' " she said, chuckling.

"Sorry?" I said. I wondered if one of her children had come in.

"Tennyson: my dove, my dear. And really, you know, he wrote some good lines. Virginia Woolf especially liked his phrase 'ancestral voices prophesying war.' Woolf's biographer tells us that she used to borrow from Tennyson's *In Memoriam*, turning the voices on her radio into the voices of ancestral urges for domination and suppression."*

I must have looked unhappy.

"That was during World War Two," she told me. "Sorry about that. Woolf was describing the voices of Hitler, Mussolini, and others of that ilk. She thought Tennyson's phrase appropriate. I only mentioned that to show you that I'm not on some sort of vendetta against poor old Tennyson. It's just that Haycock couldn't bear any suggestion that Tennyson was other than the perfect, the last, the only *real* poet; nothing, no one since. We have a chap in the department who thinks that way about Freud, which is even worse sometimes. That's the

---

*Hermione Lee, *Virginia Woolf* (London: Chalto and Windus, 1996), p. 726.

problem, you see. They don't realize or interpret their fear and disdain for women; they just think women aren't as good as men and don't belong. The young ones, of course, even the young professors without tenure . . . well, they're cute, and any man worth his salt likes having them around, but when it comes to being a permanent member of the department . . ."

I decided to put up some resistance, or at least some stiff questions, always a good way to encourage information that might otherwise be unstated or only reluctantly offered.

"God knows it isn't easy for women in the police force; I've seen enough to know that. And even among lawyers there's a lot of, well, disgusting behavior. And women don't get the big positions, though they often deserve them, and it's always assumed their bodies are always available for comment and judgment—I know all that. But there's something here that's, well, let's say you're helping but I'm not sure I altogether get it."

"Woody, don't let it worry you. No one outside of academia 'gets it.' Any person in a position like mine— or worse, who tries to explain all the nastiness and details and disregarding of bylaws and principles—ends up sounding like a nut. It's all so hard to pin down, to make clear, to demonstrate. That's what made the M.I.T. report such big news. No one before, let alone a male university president, had admitted any such situation. So don't worry if you're just puzzled and a little anxious about me; subtle discrimination is the hardest kind to describe or grasp if you haven't experienced it, and academic discrimination is the hardest to make explicable. The acts of discrimination are subtle and impossible to demonstrate. The *New York Times* had an editorial on the subject; I'll show it to you if you like."

"Is this discrimination bad enough to account for Haycock's murder?"

"Probably not. It's also worth remembering that Haycock was not widely, or even narrowly, loved by anyone. His male colleagues hardly thought him a prize, even apart from his Tennyson mania, but they knew they could control him. No one, no change they didn't want, would get by him; they could count on that. And you know about his adoring family." She sighed. "Forgive the sarcasm," she said. "A stupid indulgence."

"But a tempting one. Professor Lansbury, Antonia, would you be willing to help me out a bit in understanding, or anyway getting a line on, the other professors in the department? I know that's probably not the thing to ask, but I am investigating a murder, and I'm having a bit of trouble getting a fix on most of the members of your department." I hoped I was sounding bewildered, and maybe a little helpless. I wanted her to help me—out of pity, if that's what would do it.

"Well, I'll try." She didn't sound happy about it.

"Let's take the women: Eileen Janeer, and Janet Graham, who teaches the novel. I know they're both assistant professors. What's your take on them?"

"They're between a rock and a hard place. If they support me, or feminism, or even object to some ruling from above, they threaten their chance for tenure. Both of them try to offer me personal support, Janet more seriously than Eileen, but that's probably because her field is nearer to my interests than are the Romantics. They're both fine, really."

I must have looked puzzled and disappointed, which I was.

"I know," she said, "that isn't much help. But one of the reasons we needed to hire someone, you, is because the whole mess is so incomprehensible. Look, if you want to know my personal opinion about my colleagues, here it is: Goldberg is a horse's ass, and would never have gotten tenure if he wasn't a sycophantic friend of the boys in power, which includes the administration and Haycock. He had and has half the qualifications of Catherine, who was turned down for tenure."

"I know who Catherine is," I said sharply. "Do go on."

"Sorry about that. This whole mess since Catherine was turned down—and now Haycock's death—it hasn't helped anyone's temper, certainly not mine." She seemed to gather herself together. "Now you know what I think of Goldberg. David Longworth is in many ways a sweet old codger who'd like you to think he's a whole lot dottier than in fact he is. He wants to be chairman, and I think he's hoping that the others will put him in under the illusion that he's a weakling they'll be able to handle; I expect they're wrong. Petrillo's a sweetie; he's incapable of swatting a fly, and is as close to sainthood as anyone I've ever met, which means, given the fate of saints, that all the guys think he's a bit of an idiot. In their book—in most of our books, I guess—anybody who isn't utterly self-centered is either a liar or a fool."

"Daniel Wanamaker?" I asked. I'd recently talked to him for a short while and had the impression of a competent guy who thought that anyone not fluent in at least three languages was deficient and certainly no scholar. I'd asked him why, therefore, he didn't vote to give Catherine Dorman tenure. He said the reason was that she was "too hipped on all this gender nonsense." He had informed me that there wasn't a major thinker in the last two centuries who even bothered to mention gender, or women if it came to that, except as objects of lust and reproduction. I hadn't cared for Wanamaker, not that my sentiments on the subject mattered a damn.

"Wanamaker's a self-satisfied pedant," Antonia said. "Sorry to be so mean about it, but the fact is, he's the living proof that reading works in their original language does not necessarily mean that you are equipped to understand the text you're working with. One of the great things about Catherine was that she could read modern texts in their original language, but she didn't say that gave her any claim to having the only right interpretations. Language is important, but being a good literary critic, a good reader, is most important of all."

"So much for Wanamaker," I said, smiling.

"It really is a pretty dismal picture, isn't it?" she said.

"Well," I said, consulting my notes, "that just leaves David Lermann."

"An angel," Antonia surprisingly said. "An eternal assistant professor angel. He got tenure when no one was looking, de facto tenure. He'd been there seven years without anyone noticing the passage of time. He's not the sort whom power-hungry types notice. They're more careful now, but they weren't quite so careful years ago. David's never published anything; he couldn't care less about politics or academic quarrels; he's a born teacher; and he loves teaching. He's told me that he can't believe he's getting paid for doing something he likes so much. He teaches huge required freshmen courses where they read the Bible, and other religious testaments, and the Greeks—drama or philosophy—and talk about values as they were questioned by the ancients. His classes get bigger and bigger, because some students take them over; they're never quite the same, and he's always buried under mounds of student papers, but teaching is a calling for him and he delights in it. If you haven't talked to him, I suggest you do."

"Do you think he disliked Haycock?"

"Of course he did, or so I assume. David doesn't love everyone; unlike Petrillo, he doesn't give everyone the automatic benefit of the doubt, though not even Petrillo has managed that with Haycock and some of his buddies. No, David Lermann makes very exact analyses of people, though he's less ready to judge them than the rest of us; I guess you could say that. You've got to see a great many different points of view if you're going to teach Socratic philosophy and the Bible."

I determined to interview Lermann. Meanwhile, I tried to think of what else to ask Antonia. She'd been as honest with me as possible—I did think that. I also felt sorry for her, sorry because she might have enjoyed what she did, had she not had all the hassle and fuss within the department to distract her and make her edgy. Anyway, she promised to help me if I thought of something else, so feeling rather incomplete and dissatisfied, I left Antonia and went in search of David Lermann.

I found him in his office, talking to a student; a long line of students sitting on the floor with their backs against the wall waited for him. Instead of waiting, I interrupted him and asked if we might meet at the finish of his student conferences. He looked at his watch, made an appointment to see me in the student coffee shop an hour hence, and returned to his discussion; I couldn't tell of what, exactly, but the student seemed pretty intense about it. Good for Lermann, I thought.

He was late turning up at the coffee shop, which I'd rather expected. I could picture him trying to disentangle himself from a student and taking a long time about it. I'd spent the intervening hour wandering around the campus and thinking. I stopped in to make appointments with the dean of faculty and the president—fortunately, with the murder of one of their professors, they could hardly refuse to see me—and then walked and thought. When the hour was up, I got directions to the student coffee shop—which turned out to be in the student center, next to the college bookstore, in which I also browsed while waiting, then got myself a cup of coffee and settled at a table in the corner. I'd noticed that the bookstore had a small section called FACULTY BOOKS, where I saw books by some of my suspects. Nothing, of course, by Lermann.

He arrived disheveled and apologetic, carrying a briefcase held together by duct tape. He saw me staring at it.

"I know, I know," he said. "My wife says it's a disgrace, and I've promised to get a new one. But it works all right. I know I won't feel happy with a new one until it looks like this." He smiled.

David Lermann was the first person I'd met on this

case, or maybe on any case, who was noticeably, plainly, unquestionably fatter than I was: a lot fatter. I've noticed that fat men have difficulty looking neat or even pulled together—more so than women, if the women have any sense of themselves and have figured out what their style is. Fat men just take male clothing and shove themselves into it. Well, it's hard to explain.

I thought it funny, odd, that Lermann was fat. I mean philosophical, lovable professors who like to teach and are devoid of ambition, you tend to think of as the long, lean type, too absentminded to eat much. So much for Central Casting.

"Can I get you a coffee?" I asked.

"That would be kind of you," he surprised me by saying, "but I think I'd prefer a Coke. I'm thirsty, and I'll enjoy getting my caffeine that way."

I got him a Coke, and each of us a Danish. I had the feeling he was hungry too; I knew I was. He bit into it gratefully, and while he was chewing I told him who I was and why I needed to talk to him.

"I know," he said after a long swig of Coke. "I wondered if you were going to overlook me because I teach only freshmen and women and don't get into department politics. I did vote for Catherine Dorman, though, but that didn't really help. I don't attend meetings of the full professors because I'm not one, but I do get to vote on tenure matters, being tenured myself."

"I find it odd to meet a college professor who really loves to teach," I said. I wondered if he wondered how I knew that, but he probably assumed it was general knowledge, which it was. "The impression I have is that most professors value only the time they can get away from teaching."

"I'm fortunate. When I used to think I would have to retire at sixty-five, which isn't that far off now"—he looked to be in his middle fifties, but I didn't contradict him—"I thought, Well, I'll get a job selling shoes or something, and I'll know that I was able to do the thing I loved to do for most of my life."

"Why shoes?" I asked.

"I think it's pretty easy to become a shoe sales-person," he said. "Particularly if you're not trying to move up to something better in that line of work. I've never learned to move up, or to want to. I figure they'd put up with me if I just went on selling shoes."

I wanted to tell him I was sorry to hear he was married, because he was the only man I'd ever met whom I could think about marrying; I could tell that even on such short notice. He'd be good to live with; not to lust after—that was more the Don Jackson type—but to live with. I wouldn't mind his taped-together briefcase; I'd like talking to him. Back to work, Woody, I reminded myself.

"Have you any thoughts on Haycock's murder?" I asked. "I know you, like everyone else Haycock knew however slightly, were at his house the day he died."

"For a short while, just from courtesy. As a matter of fact, we discussed retsina."

"You did?" I said, really surprised.

"Yes. He asked me if I thought the ancient Greeks drank retsina, if Socrates drank it; I wanted to say the answer was probably yes, but that I thought that hemlock probably tasted better. I had to tell him I didn't know of a direct reference to it in Greek literature."

"Do you read Greek?" I asked, sounding more astonished than was polite.

"Oh, yes," he said. "I read Hebrew too, and I'm studying Arabic. You can't really understand these matters if you can't read them in the original tongue. Not that I don't think they should be taught by people who don't know the languages. It's just the way I feel personally."

"Don't you think they should promote someone who reads Greek?" I said.

He laughed, but decided to explain to me how easy Greek was to learn.

"But it's an entirely different alphabet," I interrupted; I did know that.

"The first year is very hard, but the great thing about learning Greek is that the second year you can read

Greek classics, some of them anyway. There's none of this 'My aunt's red pencil box' about it."

"Maybe I'll try one day," I said. "But about Haycock."

"Not a good man. It has been said, and truthfully, that you can judge a man or woman by his or her enemies; true enough, but you can also tell a thing or two about a man who has only enemies. I hope his mother and father loved him, because I really don't think anyone else did. What a sad testimony."

"You believe that he caused a great deal of harm in the department then?"

"Oh, yes; I don't suppose the English department will become heaven on earth with him gone, but it can only get better. I'm sorry to have to say it."

"Did you drink the retsina at Haycock's party?"

"I wanted to—that's the strange thing. I was about to ask him if I might have a taste when someone distracted him, and he drank it and was dead. He pointed to me and said, 'Red shirt' before he collapsed, looking straight at me. I wasn't wearing a red shirt."

"That's an effect of digoxin," I said. "Color changes. That was a narrow escape you had."

"So I have learned. I have never much feared dying, although the body fears it. But between Haycock and me, I really think the world can better spare Haycock. I wouldn't say that about many people."

We went on chatting for a bit, but there wasn't much

else to ask. He had really handed me the most dramatic revelation of the whole case. It didn't solve anything, but it shook one up.

I took out my cell phone and called Don Jackson on his cell phone to tell him I was through. He was caught up in some work, so we didn't get to meet before I set off for home, bracing myself for the wait at the Holland Tunnel entrance.

CHAPTER ELEVEN

Like a tale of little meaning, though the words are
strong.
                              —Tennyson, "The Lotos-Eaters"

Back to New Jersey the next day, later in the morning with the tunnel less crowded. I had appointments with the president of the college and the dean, in that order. I wasn't hoping for much, but I had to try. Don had agreed to meet for an early dinner at "our" place, which allowed me to avoid the evening rush hour and to see him again. Maybe even give him a lift on my bike. Well, I enjoyed it, and who else knew or cared?

The president kept me waiting for the obligatory quarter of an hour. If you see people on time (unless they're wealthy donors or likely to be, in which case I suppose you wait for them on the threshold) you lose face. I've never understood this, and make a point of being on time if I can, since I appreciate promptness in others. One of the reasons I ride a bike is because, aside from rush hour to and from New Jersey, I can pretty well figure how long the trip will take me and arrive on the dot or as near as makes no matter.

I was finally ushered into his presence by the sort of secretary who asks if you want tea or coffee. I refused; I wouldn't dream of asking Octavia to make tea or coffee, though sometimes if she's having it herself she'll offer me some, and vice versa. I wasn't with the president for more than five minutes before it became clear that he didn't know anything about the Haycock murder, except that it had occurred, and he certainly didn't know anything about the situation in the English department. That, apparently, wasn't his job, although he didn't say so. He fudged and dodged, and as far as I was concerned declared himself thoroughly useless. I gathered his responsibility was the larger picture: the infrastructure, meaning the buildings and what was holding them up, and institutional finances, meaning raising money. He was good at that—I'd already been told that was his chief, perhaps only talent—and while he didn't exactly brush me off, I got the message that there was little point in wasting his time or mine. Since I agreed with this, I made my exit as soon as I could without being dismissive; I felt dismissive toward him.

The dean was quite another matter. The faculty and students, as well as the curriculum, were his responsibility, and he certainly knew what was what in the English department. I was bowed into his presence by the same class of secretary—clearly smart and probably more knowledgeable than her boss, a characteristic I had gathered of most of the administrative staff.

"I don't know how I can help you," he began, not too promisingly. "The whole situation has been mind-boggling. I mean, why should anyone want to murder Charles Haycock?"

I was in no mood for evasive bullshit.

"Please, Dean," I said. "You know as well as I and no doubt a good many other people do that Professor Haycock was a troublemaker and, to say the least, a difficult colleague. What would help me is your view of the situation."

"Really, Miss—Ms.—Woodhaven, I can hardly discuss confidential college matters with you."

"Ah, but you can and must, Dean," I said. I stood up and leaned against his desk, looking down at him. I'm rather a large object to have directly in your line of vision, a fact I make good use of when necessary. "You may recall that the police are also investigating this matter, working with me—that is, we are working together. I would hate to have to get a search warrant and go through all your files, but if I have to I will. Now wouldn't it be easier for all of us if you just tell me what you know about Professor Haycock and the troubles in the English department and give me any relevant documents?" I didn't make it sound exactly like a question.

The dean was flustered, as I had hoped he would be. If I involved the police, or made a noisy fuss of any sort, he would be in the spotlight, and who knew where that might lead? He had to decide, and quickly, whether it was better to play along with me or keep dodging. I decided to give his dilemma a spin in my direction.

"I have an appointment with the police later today. I'll get that warrant if I have to, and come back with official company." I saw no point in mentioning that my appointment with the police was in order to eat a hamburger and maybe have one beer. I paused meaningfully. And I could see it working.

"In fact, Professor Haycock was causing a certain amount of discomfort in his department and, by obvious extension, in the administration. He seemed to think he would be able and should be allowed to transform the department into something nearer to his own idea of literary studies."

"Did he tell you that?"

"Yes, he told me, he wrote me, he harangued me. He seemed determined to make life unpleasant for anyone who didn't, well, agree to go his way. Not," the dean quickly added, "that his actions or desires were a motive for murder; hardly that, of course. Still, well . . ."

"Life will be a lot simpler now that he's gone, however he went," I finished for him.

"I would hesitate to put it that way," he said. "I think you're viewing the whole affair in an unfortunate and dramatic light."

I forbore to point out that murder was by definition dramatic. "And were you at his party where the fatal drink was taken?" I asked. I knew he wasn't, but it never hurts to make the person you're questioning uneasy, especially if he's what they call a hostile witness—especially if he's a dean.

"I was two thousand miles away, at a conference in Phoenix, Arizona, as it happens," he said.

"Exactly why your view of the situation is so important to me then," I said. Flattery works too. "Almost everyone else even remotely connected to this case was there. The insights of someone who wasn't there and who knows the college are invaluable. Surely you can see that." I sat back in my chair and looked expectant.

"Haycock was really serious about reorganizing the department. He had a few colleagues who would go along with him, but on the whole his plan would have been disruptive, to say the least. When he died, I had been planning to put the matter before the president and then take some action. Exactly what action I can't say; in fact," he added, sensing my question, "I don't know. And that's all I can tell you about it. I'm sure the situation would have been resolved without too much fuss. Professors often begin by suggesting extreme measures; that gives them maneuvering room."

"Did you know that he was particularly antagonistic to Professor Lansbury, Antonia Lansbury?"

"My dear Ms. Woodhaven, everyone knew that; I suspect even the groundspeople knew that. She and some others—junior people, I believe—put on some play that Haycock found exceedingly offensive. I didn't see it and don't know what it was. In any case, they were at loggerheads; I don't think they agreed on anything. But do try to understand, that kind of enmity is, alas, not unusual in academic departments, even in a relatively small college like this. It never leads to violence. I would advise you not to make too much of it."

"I'll try not to," I said. He looked at his watch, and the phone rang to tell him his next appointment was waiting.

"I don't want to rush you," he said, clearly dying to, "but I have another appointment. Perhaps Miss Dubinsky, my secretary, can help you if you need any more information."

I could have kissed him. I wanted to question the secretary, and now he gave me the right to do so with fewer lies necessary. For once in this case, it seemed, the gods were on my side. He rose to show me out, and to greet a small committee of what I took to be trustees or something; they looked rather too spick-and-span for faculty these days.

I greeted "Miss" Dubinsky and, giving my name and occupation, held out my hand. She took it rather dubiously; I gather hands were not usually offered to her. "I hope you can help me, as the dean has suggested you might. Since he had to meet with those folks"—I pointed to his closed office door—"he said that you would be glad to assist me in any way you could."

She looked uneasy, in need of persuasion. "It's no great thing," I said soothingly. "I assured the dean there was no need to get a search warrant from the police, with whom I am working on this investigation. All I need to see is the letter Professor Haycock of the English department wrote to the dean suggesting changes in the department's structure." I tried to sound a trifle bored with the whole thing, but mindful of my duties.

"Well," she said, "if the dean said you could see it." She walked slowly to the file cabinet, still not quite sure, but began to rifle through the files. "I don't think I should let you take it away," she said. "You'll have to read it here."

"Of course," I agreed at once, taking the letter—it took some restraint not to grab it from her—and reading it where I was, standing, so as not to appear too eager or intent. It was a long letter—two full pages—and I read the first page twice before turning to the second, which I also read twice. I had to commit it to memory, and I didn't want to appear to be studying it too carefully. I'm a fast reader, but you would never have known it from the pace with which I worked my way through that letter.

The letter really showed what a nut Haycock was. His long-range plan was to fire all the untenured types, including the writing guy, Kevin Oakwood, who had certainly misunderstood Haycock's view of him. Then he wanted to force all the tenured professors who didn't suit his fancy—that wasn't how he put it, of course, but I knew the cast of characters—to teach only required survey and composition courses. No wonder someone had decided to murder him; the only wonder was that he hadn't died sooner. The question was, of course, who had decided to murder him?

None of my astonishment or pleasure at the revelation this letter offered appeared on my face or was revealed by my slow, lazy movements. Holy cat, I thought, a phrase I hadn't used since I was too young to know swear words. (Funny, really, how the usual nasty epithets have become so overused that the innocent swear words of one's youth carry new emphasis.) Easy does it, Woody, I said to myself. Hand the lady—I was sure she would have been pleased to be called a lady—back the letter, smile in a bored but gracious sort of way, and leave before the dear dean discovers what you've read. "Nice to have met you, and many thanks for your help," I said casually but politely, and departed.

But I hadn't quite made it out of the building when my cell phone rang. It took me a few minutes to realize that the ringing was coming from my bag and was my new phone. Feeling ridiculously flustered, I put my bag down and rummaged in it for the phone, which kept on ringing. I hoped to get it before five rings, when my message to please leave a message would come on. I barely made it, but managed to push the right button and say "Hello" into the damn thing.

"Woody," the voice said. It was Don Jackson. "Are you finished with the administration yet?"

"Just finished," I said, looking around as other people in the corridor stared at me. I found myself flushing because I had reacted so badly to people I passed on the street shouting into cell phones and talking chitchat as though walking and thinking weren't sufficient activity for a person. I also resented having their phone voices intrude on my thoughts. To say nothing of those who drove while talking on the phone, which a few old acquaintances from my lawyer days told me were causing a lot of accidents. Then there were those who talked on trains, bothering tired commuters who wanted quiet. There was even a plan—

"You there, Woody?"

"I'm here—trying to get used to this damn thing. Is there a problem about supper?"

"There's a problem on the campus where you are; I'm on my way. Do you know some guy named Kevin Oakwood?"

"Not to say *know*. I've listened while he drank beer and talked."

"Good enough. Well, he's just beaten up a professor in the English department."

"Really?" I said. "Which one?" I was torn between hope and anxiety. Anxiety won.

"His name is Petrillo. Mr. Oakwood seems to have knocked him about pretty badly. They've called an ambulance."

"Where was all this?" It occurred to me how sheltered the dean's office—and the president's, of course—were from outbreaks elsewhere on the campus.

"Near the building with the English department. Just step outside of wherever you are; you can't miss it. A big crowd, I gather. Meet me there."

And he was gone. Perhaps people signed off cell phones faster than the usual kind, where, if you weren't hanging up on someone, you managed to say goodbye in a friendly way. I left the building and saw that Don was right. One could hardly miss the crowd outside standing around as though they were watching a prizefight. Which, I told myself, in a way they had been.

Once there I found the student Mr. Ferguson shouting with the rest. Pulling him aside, I demanded a report on what had happened. The police were on their way, though without sirens. Apparently they respected the quiet of this bucolic college too much for that. Mustn't frighten the students. From what I could see, the students were enjoying themselves and unlikely to be frightened by anything. An ambulance was also on its way, its siren going full blast, paying, I was relieved to see, no attention to the niceties influencing the police.

I looked demandingly at Mr. Ferguson. "I don't know," he said. "I wasn't here at the beginning, though I came in during the worst of it. What can I tell you? That guy"—he pointed to Kevin Oakwood, who was being restrained by two policemen—"was beating up Professor Petrillo. Maybe he didn't like medieval literature any more than I did."

"I don't think this is funny," I said, scowling.

"I know. But why would anyone want to beat up Petrillo? I mean, he's a really nice guy; what harm could he do anyone? It isn't even as though this was a student who'd been failed in a course. Maybe the guy was drunk."

Having spent all the time I had talking with Kevin Oakwood in a bar, I thought that very likely. He had obviously possessed a quick temper, restrained with difficulty. Although I didn't say this to Mr. Ferguson (I reminded myself to ask him his first name), I thought the likely scenario was that Petrillo had interfered between Oakwood and a female student with whom Oakwood was doing whatever Oakwood did with students. That seemed the likeliest explanation and fit in with both their characters as I had observed them.

The ambulance men had gathered up Professor Petrillo, who really looked the worse for wear. I heard one of the students in the crowd tell another that Oakwood had been kicking his opponent once he was on the ground; clearly poor Petrillo was in really bad shape.

The police did their best to disperse the crowd as the ambulance pulled out. I saw Don there then, taking names and talking to witnesses. I managed to get near enough to Don to exchange glances with him. "See you as arranged," he said, so I gathered he would be able to make supper. If not, he could always call me on the cell phone, whose uses I was beginning to appreciate.

After you've read an outlandish letter in the dean's office and seen a brutal fight, or anyway the tag end of it, it's a little hard to think what to do next. But Mr. Ferguson was still nearby, so I asked him if he would introduce me to other students in the crowd from the English department. "And by the way," I said, "what's your first name? Mine's Woody."

"Alan," he said. "But most people call me Cap." He

reached over and grabbed a nearby guy. "This here's Phil," he said. "Takes English courses like the rest of us, but not a major. Will he do?"

Phil glared at Cap, but Cap explained I was a private eye with a motorbike who wanted to talk to English students, which seemed to calm him down. "Any others here?" Cap asked.

"Some girls," Phil said, after looking me over. "You want them?"

I nodded and turned to Cap. "How did you know I was a private eye?" I asked.

"Oh, shit, everybody knows," he said. "You can't be much of a private eye around here if you don't know how a college grapevine works. Shit, Woody, I found out you were a private eye ten minutes after I met you. Well, ten minutes after I looked over your wheels."

I realized I had fallen in his estimation, and was sorry about that. But at that moment Phil returned with two girls in tow, both of them talking at once. "They were here from the beginning," Phil said, jerking his thumb toward the girls.

"You were here when it started?" I asked them hopefully. They had been, and speaking contrapuntally, occasionally correcting each other, they told me all they could remember of it. We stood around when most of the others had gone, but though I heard them through, and asked lots of questions, and although Cap and Phil joined in the description from the moment they had come upon the scene, I wasn't exactly left with a clear picture of what had happened, except that the two men had met, the girls thought by accident, and Oakwood had screamed "You goddamn fucking fool," and leaped on Petrillo.

"It was horrible," the girls assured me. I gathered that Petrillo was plainly not a fighter, had tried to reason with Oakwood and ask him what the matter was, which had only seemed to infuriate Oakwood further. He punched Petrillo in the face, and when Petrillo didn't get up again, he began kicking him. "It was horrible," was the refrain of their account. Phil and Cap had arrived by this time, and were a little more descriptive of the fight moves they had witnessed.

"It was exactly as though he, Oakwood, had been sent by someone to beat Petrillo up and teach him a lesson," Phil said. "You know, you borrow money from the mob, you don't pay up, or you don't pay your gambling debts, first they beat you up as a warning, and the next time they kill you. This was the beating. That's the way it looked to me."

"I agree with that," Cap said. The young women nodded their heads as though once it was explained to them the explanation fit what they had seen.

I hardly thought Petrillo owed Oakwood or anyone else money, but there was something about the description that fit Oakwood as I had observed him. Not that he was likely to be a thug working for gamblers, but he seemed to me the sort who might enjoy beating people up and who might have some practice at it. But why Petrillo? It was only slowly that I realized Phil and Cap had been referring to scenes in movies, but they were scenes they thought more than likely to occur in real life. And when it came right down to it, so did I. We lived in violent times, even on a pleasant college campus.

I felt a bit ashamed of the fact that I regretted having missed the fight, having arrived just too late for the action. I'm not bloodthirsty, really I'm not, and I dislike enactments of male violence. But I couldn't help suspecting that any clue to what went on between those two ill-matched men might have been evident at the start of the fight, but by now was probably lost or in need of being painfully dug out, with little hope of complete success.

Between Haycock's letter and this fight, the plot was getting more complex but hardly providing any clues to the murder. Haycock was hated; not all the members of the English department loved one another, to put it mildly, but how did that account for murder? If Petrillo had murdered Haycock, and Oakwood had loved Haycock, their fight might make sense. But it didn't make sense. Probably poor Petrillo had said something provoking to Oakwood, who was hardly one to restrain his violent, aggressive impulses.

I decided to go over to the local hospital, where they had taken Petrillo. Maybe he would talk to me; maybe I would find out something. But by the time I had reached my bike and made it to the hospital, I was told that Petrillo had been moved to a larger "medical facility" where they had CAT scans, MRIs, and all the rest of it. I asked if that meant he was in critical condition, but they weren't telling me anything. I would have to wait and see if Don had learned more; the police were better at extracting information from hospitals than I could hope to be. I felt bad about Petrillo, a nice guy, and hardly able to defend himself against brutal fists and feet.

My next move was to pursue the fists and feet to the police station, where Oakwood was in jail, or so I assumed. I doubted they'd let me see him either, but you have to keep on trying. You never know.

As it turned out, my instincts were correct. Don Jackson was there, and agreed to let me interview Oakwood, or at least sit in on Don's interview with him.

"No point getting you into hot water," I said, giving in to my conscience and defying my investigative urges. This wasn't altogether out of consideration for Don or my feelings for him. If the police had anything against me it wouldn't help me much in the end.

But Don said not to worry. "They know you're investigating the murder, and they're as anxious as you are to have it solved. As I suggested earlier"—and he grinned at me—"they're particularly eager for you to solve it. Less backlash at them. So let's go."

Oakwood was in a cell. They didn't seem to have interview rooms here, or not one available, or maybe they just wanted to make him feel locked up, but we interviewed him in the cell. That meant Don and I both stood, while Oakwood sat on his bunk and scowled.

"What the fuck is she doing here?" he said to Don. "I already talked to fatty here, and I don't need to talk with her again."

"I'll ask the questions," Don said. "You answer them and otherwise shut up. Do I make myself clear?" This last question was accompanied by Don's making himself bigger and taller, which of course he already was—big and tall, I mean. I knew the trick: if you're large, use it. I guess Oakwood had had enough physical activity for the day, because he backed down at once.

"I have nothing to tell you," he said, but in a quieter way. "The guy pissed me off and I have a short fuse; so convict me of assault, which can't be a felony all the way at the top of the alphabet, and tell me what the bail is."

Don didn't explain that he had all his facts wrong about the process; he just asked, "What did Professor Petrillo say that bothered you?"

"Oh, some stupid thing, something against writers

who teach because they can't write—something like that."

"That doesn't sound like Petrillo," I said. "That's not the kind of thing he would say. It's totally out of character."

I hadn't planned to speak, but Don didn't know Petrillo even as well as I did, and I thought it worth making the point that Petrillo was the least likely of anyone I had ever encountered to say something pointedly unkind. One thing about Petrillo: nastiness wasn't in his nature.

"Okay," Don said. "Try again, Oakwood."

"I'm through talking," Oakwood said. "I beat the guy up. You've got plenty of witnesses, so why should I deny it? Let's just say I hate professors who have too easy lives, too many vacations, and too little real work. Will that hold you?"

Without another look at Oakwood, Don called for the guard, who opened the cell door. We parted in silence, a silence I hoped Oakwood would regard as ominous. I thought it was a good move of Don's. We weren't going to get anything more, and the more Don asked, the more reason Oakwood had to dig himself in and elaborate on his lie, or just keep repeating it.

Outside the station, Don told me that the police were asking all the students who had witnessed the fight and given their names to the police—and there were many—how the fight began. But he didn't have much hope of learning anything new.

"My guess," Don said, "is that he had worked up his anger at Petrillo before they happened to meet, and meeting him was enough to set off the explosion. But we have to see what else we can find. Are we still meeting as agreed?"

I assured him that we were, and went off to the coffee shop to think. First, of course, I called Octavia on my cell phone. It was nice, I had to admit, not to have to track down a public phone, not to have to find the money or my charge card, and not to find the public phone broken, as they so often were. I was generous enough to tell all this to Octavia when I reached her.

Octavia merely grunted. "Just remember to carry an extra battery," she said. "They don't last forever. You don't want the phone to fail when you need it most."

"Thanks for the advice," I said formally. Sometimes Octavia gets ahead of herself. But of course, I would carry a spare battery from now on. The most annoying thing about Octavia is that she's so often right. I ask you, what's more annoying than that?

CHAPTER TWELVE

That which we are, we are.
—Tennyson, "Ulysses"

At supper, over the only beer I could allow myself, Don told me that all the stories the police had gathered from the fight's onlookers were similar, and similarly uninformative. He said only one was different, and he wasn't sure what it meant, if anything.

"One girl was passing by there at the actual moment when Oakwood accosted Petrillo," Don said between bites. "She said he leaped on Petrillo, who hadn't even seen Oakwood coming. And while he leaped, according to this girl, Oakwood shouted, 'You better learn to shut up, you pompous religious shit.' The girl was so shocked by his words that she seemed to have stood there transfixed while Oakwood was punching Petrillo. And then she began to scream, and other people crowded around, and eventually someone called the security guards, and the security guards called the police. Obviously the security guards felt they couldn't handle the fight and the crowd, and that's a strong indication of

213

the degree of violence. Police are called onto the campus unwillingly, and only when it's the case of danger from a person 'not a member of the campus community,' as they put it."

"They probably thought Oakwood was a thug from the big, mean outside world," I said. There may be something better than a hamburger and a beer, but I don't know what it is. But it was finished; I could have eaten and drunk it all over again, but some restraint in life is to be encouraged. I waved at the waitress and asked for coffee. "And," I added, having partly subdued my hunger, "in a sense they were right: Oakwood was an outsider."

"I sent his prints and description through the system. No record."

"I said he was an outsider, not a career criminal."

"I'd be very surprised if he hadn't assaulted someone before, maybe many someones. That beating he gave Petrillo was not a first try."

I told Don what Cap and Phil had said about how the attack had struck them. "It's all very well to say that they'd seen too many movies, but movies not only reflect real violence, they encourage imitations."

Don nodded. There was no need to elaborate on that point. We both thanked whatever gods there are that no guns had been involved. In a violent society like America, with guns as easy to come by as cigarettes, it's a miracle if anyone these days resorts to his fists and leaves it at that. We despised Oakwood for attacking Petrillo, and praised him for being an old-fashioned, weaponless bully. It's a crazy world, all right.

"What do you think Oakwood meant about telling Petrillo to shut up? What had he been blabbing about?"

Of course, as I told Don, I'd been wondering about that myself. There was no doubt Petrillo was a bit, well, sanctimonious in the way he talked about sin, and maybe he'd just gotten on Oakwood's nerves. Or maybe, and I thought this more likely, a female student had talked to Petrillo about Oakwood's having come on to her, and Petrillo had confronted Oakwood, who'd seethed for a while, and his short fuse had reached the exploding point. Around then, I guess, poor Petrillo happened along. But they were bound to meet sooner or later.

"By the way," I asked Don, after we'd both thought about this for a while, "did you look into the students who were serving at Haycock's party the day he was killed?"

"It was on the top of my list to report on that," Don said, smiling. "And I would have if we hadn't been distracted by the latest outbreak."

"Are you suggesting it had anything to do with the murder?"

"No. I only meant a murder and a beating on this

campus in one semester . . . well, one does notice the timing."

"I know. The only problem is, Oakwood is not a nice person, which I figured out in my one short conversation with him—if you could call it a conversation; it was more just Oakwood revealing his unpleasant nature."

"Right. There wasn't anything unusual about the students. One of them was a substitute—the girl Oakwood told you he knew, in fact. She had asked the girl who got called for the job if she could go instead. She said she needed the money, and the other girl agreed. They were used to doing this sort of favor for each other. Nothing bad known about the girl who served at the party, unless you count the fact that she seems to have put up with Oakwood. Do you think it means anything?"

"Probably not," I said, sighing. "Nothing in this damn case means anything." It was true. There were all sorts of promising leads, all trailing off into nothing. I was wishing we could nab Oakwood for Haycock's murder. He was the only person I'd met from either the English department or the guest list who seemed to me capable of murder, capable even of delighting in it. But poison seemed to require a bit too much planning for him. Also I couldn't really imagine his dropping eight or more pills into the bottle of retsina with nobody noticing. He couldn't do anything without everybody noticing. Beating or bludgeoning was more his style. I told Don what I was thinking.

"I know," he said. "We've been thinking along all the same lines, which is how anyone with two brains to rub together would think about the evidence we have. The fact is, Woody, it was probably one of those professors of English literature who'd never done anything like that before and never will again. Probably someone who's read a lot of detective stories and was able to make a plan about what he or she had learned. Isn't that how you figure it?"

"Exactly," I said. I looked at my watch. "Time I pushed off," I told him. "Maybe we could call and find out how poor Petrillo's doing."

"I think he's all right, not seriously injured, though they need to keep him for a while. Some of his organs got a bit bruised, but they weren't badly damaged. That can happen. And he has a couple of broken ribs from being kicked, and his face is a mess. We're really going to get Oakwood on aggravated assault. The college wants us to take him off their hands, so he'll get what's coming to him. I'll stop by and see Petrillo tomorrow, but I don't think there's much he can tell us. As far as he was concerned, the whole thing was out of the blue, without reason."

"There must have been a reason, or what Oakwood considered a reason," I said.

"Sure. But that doesn't mean Petrillo knows what it is."

"No," I said. "Probably not. Will you call me tomorrow and let me know what you learn from Petrillo, or what you don't learn?"

"Of course," Don said as we left the restaurant. I was feeling at a loose end, as my mother used to say, everything hanging in the air. I dropped Don off at the police station and set out for home. It had been a long, if inconclusive day.

The next day I had an invitation from Kate Fansler, who asked if I would like to stop by in the late afternoon. She would certainly understand if I couldn't, but would welcome me if I found it convenient.

I found it more than convenient: enticing. I needed to talk to someone about the case, someone who had most of the background and just needed filling in on the most recent events—my meeting with the dean and the dean's secretary, and the brutal encounter between Oakwood and poor Petrillo.

At Kate's insistence, I told her about these matters— after greeting Banny, of course, and accepting a drink. Kate listened intently, and then suggested that we put off discussing it until she could tell me about the more or less Tennysonian fun she had been having.

"I've been reading *Freshwater*," she said. "It really is a hoot." I must have looked blank because she held up the slender book.

"Ah," I said as the penny dropped. "The play they put on that so upset Haycock. But of course everything upset Haycock. Why is it called *Freshwater*? I suppose I ought to know," I added gloomily.

Kate ignored this. "Freshwater was the house on the Isle of Wight owned by Mrs. Cameron, who was Virginia Woolf's aunt and a great photographer. Tennyson had a house nearby. Do listen to this. In the play, Tennyson is talking to Ellen Terry, who would become a famous actor but who was, at the moment, the very young, unhappy wife of the painter Watts, decades her senior. She is flirting with Tennyson, who says to her: 'You should see me in my bath! I have thighs like alabaster!' " Kate looked at me expectantly.

"Was there something wrong with his thighs?" I asked.

"Oh, dear," Kate said. "No, I don't think there was anything wrong. It's just not the sort of remark one expects from so famous a Victorian poet. Clearly Virginia Woolf, who wrote the play, felt great affection for Tennyson, but to Haycock this must have seemed like the cruelest and most unnecessary mockery."

I slid down further into my chair, took a swig of my

drink, and tried to look happy. Kate decided to have one more shot at convincing me of whatever she was trying to convince me of.

"Well, then, listen to this. Tennyson is talking to Mrs. Cameron, who has been posing a donkey, who was supposed to be carrying St. Christopher on its back; Mrs. Cameron liked to make allegorical pictures. She mentions the ass to Tennyson, who says:

> Yes, there was a damned ass praising Browning the other day. Browning, I tell you. But could Browning have written: "The moan of doves in immemorial elms, / The murmuring of innumerable bees." Or this, perhaps the loveliest line in the language—"The mellow ouzel fluting on the lawn."

There was a pause. "Kate," I said, in what I hoped was a pathetic tone, "I'm not quite sure what you're getting at."

"Because you don't know what an ouzel is," Kate said. "No one but Tennyson knew before he wrote that line. He liked to use odd words from Middle English. I think it's a kind of water bird."

"It's not just the ouzel," I said. "It's all of it. I'm sorry to be such a disappointment, Kate."

Kate put the book down with a sigh, and then I thought of my conversation with Rick Fowler. "I do remember something," I said. "Something about 'thump, thump, thump.' "

Kate brightened up. "That's 'Alice'," she said. "A take-off on 'Maud' and the fact that the flowers in Tennyson's poem talked." Kate looked at the ceiling and recited:

There has fallen a splendid tear
From the passion-flower at the gate.
She is coming, my dove, my dear;
She is coming, my life, my fate;
The red rose cries, "She is near she is near";
And the white rose weeps, "She is late";
The Larkspur listens. "I hear, I hear";
And the lily whispers, "I wait."

There was a pause. "Well," I finally said, "no one can accuse *you* of not liking Tennyson, and you say they couldn't accuse Virginia Woolf of not liking him either. I can't see what Haycock was all wrought up about."

"That's it, you see. Woolf's comedy is all good, clean fun, not meant to injure or mock anyone. That it got under Haycock's skin suggests he may have been, to put it mildly, a bit off balance. And it's not that I really appreciate Tennyson. I had an aging professor in college— she was probably not much older than I am now, but she seemed ancient to me then—and she used to quote Tennyson with relish. We found her funny, of course, but we also saw that her affection for his poetry was profound, particularly for 'Maud.' Those are the only lines I remember, if you want to know."

I couldn't think what to say. I took another sip and just sat there, waiting. Maybe everyone who taught literature went a bit nuts from time to time. That would certainly explain a lot. Kate seemed to be still thinking of talking flowers or something. Slowly I got my mind back into gear.

"We don't need Virginia Woolf or anyone else to tell us Haycock was peculiar and obsessed with Tennyson," I said. "But where does that get us? I mean, do you think he meant to kill Antonia or all of those who put on *Freshwater*, but got mixed up and drank the retsina before offering it to them?"

"I don't think we should put too much emphasis on Tennyson," Kate said. I thought she had a nerve, frankly. Who'd been quoting him about larkspurs and passion-flowers? "Was the dean at that party of Haycock's?"

"No. He was in Arizona at some conference."

"Haycock was certainly giving him a lot of misery. Maybe he hired someone?"

"I've thought of that. Do you really think a dean could set out to murder a professor?"

"I'm sure a lot of them would like to. I'm hardly unbiased, but I find it easier to imagine a dean doing that than a professor, however unhappy."

"Kate, I really have trouble believing that academics, professors, can behave as crazily as these seem to do, at least some of them. I know Oakwood is only an adjunct, but how many teachers of writing beat people to a pulp?"

"I'll tell you something I heard just the other day," Kate said. "This wasn't an English department, but the situation isn't all that different. In this case, the head of the department, who was in tight with the administration, took petty revenge on any faculty member who disagreed with him, even in a reasonable way. He would take away courses, or find some way to pay them back. So nobody disagreed with him, and there was no point in trying to move him out of the chair because he would still have his in with the boys in central administration."

"Did anyone try to murder him?"

"No. I was right when I said murder was very seldom if ever resorted to in the academic world. But members of the department have started leaving, and at some point the administration may catch on. Or they may not, of course. The point, Woody, is that petty tyrants exist everywhere, and no less in academia."

"I guess they're not so petty."

"True, they're not Saddam Hussein. And their revenge is usually in the petty things that can make a professor miserable. Of course, Saddam Hussein murdered his son-in-law, so maybe Haycock is more like that."

"Kate," I said. "We've gone from a play called *Freshwater* to Saddam Hussein, and I have the feeling I'm not exactly making any progress. About this play, for instance. Has it ever been put on? Except by Rick and Antonia and their friends at the college?"

"You mean professionally? No. It was just written for a birthday party. And it was really a group project. We tend to read what Woolf wrote and concentrate on that, but the costumes and the setting and the acting were all just as important to the Bloomsbury group when they put it on."

"It wasn't in a theatre?"

"No, it was in Vanessa Bell's studio. They were all talented, and they liked pooling their talents and having fun, which they certainly did on that occasion. Don't worry about *Freshwater*, Woody. Have another drink."

I accepted with thanks. But I couldn't get over the fact that none of this, however intriguing to literary types like Kate and Antonia, was throwing any light on the murder. I thought of saying this and then decided to drink up and depart. Not that I blamed Kate for not coming up with something. What could she possibly have come up with, knowing what I knew and lots of poetry besides? She couldn't pluck a solution out of the air. I did rather want to ask Kate what Reed had done for Don Jackson to make him so nice to me, and not at all like the usual policeman, but it wasn't any of my business. I knew that if I asked Kate or Reed, they would say that Don would tell me if he wanted to. That's what I would have said under the circumstances.

After a while I left. Once I was out of the building, I started muttering to myself about larkspurs and lilies. I went home on the subway and took a long, hot bath.

I was back in New Jersey the next day. Don had agreed to meet me and tell me about Petrillo and what he said, if anything. Somehow tearing out to Jersey and talking with Don gave me the sensation of doing something, though I knew damn well I wasn't doing anything, and the way I felt now, probably never would—not with this case. I tried to calm myself with the thought that Haycock was really a nut, that the college, his family, and everyone else would be better off without him, and that some crimes never get solved and this, obviously, was going to be one of them. But I still don't believe that anyone has the right to take another person's life, and I also didn't think they should get away with it. Well, Woody, I told myself, win some, lose some.

Don and I met in the restaurant, of course. It

was lunchtime, and food or coffee or booze, if available, makes it easier to talk. I particularly like talking in a restaurant booth. You feel private in a booth, not like people at the next table might find your conversation more interesting than theirs. Booths are cozy. I had mentioned this to Don once, and he thought so too, so it was a natural place for us to meet.

"I saw Petrillo," Don said. "Most of the faculty had come to see him, though they could stay only for a minute. And everyone seems to have sent flowers, and his students sent notes. He's clearly a man for whom people have a lot of affection."

"Maybe that's what got under Oakwood's skin."

"Among other things, I guess. I did get to talk to Petrillo. I asked him if he knew what was bothering Oakwood, and why Oakwood had said what he did, about shutting up. Petrillo said he'd thought about that a lot, lying still, with his head and everything else hurting, and feeling drowsy from the painkillers they'd given him, and he'd decided that he'd never figure out what was troubling Oakwood. That was his word: 'troubling.' Then he said, 'I guess I just got on his nerves; I do get on people's nerves sometimes.' There didn't seem much else to say, so I left. Petrillo is a genuinely sweet guy, if you want my opinion."

"Mine too," I said. "Did you get the impression at all, even faintly, that he might have known what Oakwood meant but had decided not to say?"

"Yes, I did. But it was a very faint impression; it was also what I wanted to think."

"Don," I said, "should we just throw in the towel? I mean, we've been over it all; I've learned more about Tennyson and about some crummy play put on by friends of Virginia Woolf and about academic politics than I ever thought I would know or need to know. And it all turns out to be spun sugar. You must see what I mean. It's not bad to lick at, even to enjoy, but it's not food; it's not substantial."

Don nodded. "You're probably right, but I don't see any need to give up just yet. Let's let it all sit for a few days. Each of us can go over it and see if any light breaks through. After that, I'm ready to call it a day when you are."

"A few days," I said. "Anyway, it was nice to meet up with you, Don, and I know that without your help, without your being ready to cooperate with me, I wouldn't have gotten this far. It helped a lot to be able to throw the authority of the police around when I wanted something, and to have someone to talk it over with."

"I liked working with you too, Woody. It started out

as a favor to Reed, but it ended up being a pleasure. At least there's that."

I didn't say anything; I didn't trust myself not to become silly, or some other damn thing. I did like Don. After the few more days we were allowing ourselves, we'd probably never meet again. Oh, maybe I could call him and say, "Hey, I'm going to Jersey; want to have a hamburger at our place?" But it was unlikely. I just kept quiet, getting a grip on myself.

"Woody," Don said, "you must have wondered what Reed could have done for me so that he had a chip to call in, a reason to ask me to help you with this investigation."

"I did wonder. But I don't need to know."

"I'll give you a brief outline. I used to be a cop in New York City. I got to know Reed when he was an assistant D.A. There was a big foul-up. I got into trouble with the other cops because I objected to their racism, to what we now call profiling: you know, if he's black and in a nice car, pull him over, maybe rough him up. There were other things; not all cops are good guys. Anyway, I didn't react very well; I went off the deep end. My marriage broke up, I drank too much, I fought with everyone. Maybe a little like Oakwood. And Reed got hold of me. We'd gotten to know each other a bit through some of the cases he had handled, and he . . . well, he showed up one day and started yelling. Screaming, telling me I was a bloody fool, and to shape up, and not to let those damn cops ruin my life for me. I started screaming back about what did he suggest, I still had to support my kids and ex-wife—well, you can imagine it. I was deep into self-pity and self-hate and on the road to God knows what. Reed said if I pulled myself together he'd help me. He got me this job here; he talked me into the benefits of small-town life; he must have pulled some strings with this police department, because they've treated me decently. I could never thank him, we never talked again, but when he asked for me to, well, watch out for you, I did it. That's about it, except that I can have my kids here for vacations and weekends, and I've discovered that how high you go is less important than how it feels going along. So that's it."

It was the longest single speech he'd ever made, and I really admired him for telling me. But I didn't want us to sit around feeling embarrassed. So I skipped right on to another topic.

"I had an idea of how they ought to have killed Haycock," I said, after we'd gotten refills on the coffee.

"Oh, you're planning murders now."

"That's it. I just learned that Viagra, you know, the drug men take—"

"I know about it," he said, smiling.

"Well, it's dangerous to take it if you've got a heart condition. Now, if the murderer had just given Haycock Viagra we'd never find out if he took it because someone wanted to kill him or because he wanted to get it up."

"That's a great plot, Woody. You ought to sell it to someone who writes those detective stories that are so popular."

"Well, remember you heard it here first," I said.

He smiled. "I'll certainly remember," he said. "Who could forget a thing like that?"

We seemed to be comfortable again, so I dropped him off at the police station, thinking as he got off the bike, Maybe someday I'll take him for a nice, long ride.

CHAPTER THIRTEEN

I meet and dole
Unequal Laws unto a savage race.
                    —Tennyson, "Ulysses"

The next morning in the office I determined to stop thinking about Don Jackson, Clifton College, and, if it came to that, all of New Jersey. Octavia had finished writing up the bills for the few finished cases we'd completed in the last weeks, and had made an appointment for me to see a new client at ten. I hoped it was not another case involving crazy academics, but I was a bit worried because all Octavia could tell me about the man coming to see me was that he sounded old rather than young, and not uneducated. Octavia's double negatives were always meaningful. This meant he might have an advanced degree or might have picked up so-called proper speech somewhere along the line, she wasn't sure which. Please let him not be an academic, I muttered, with no idea of whom I was addressing.

But my prayer, if that's what it was, was heard. The man who introduced himself was, he told me, a lawyer with a particularly delicate problem. I nodded encouragingly. "I must be assured of absolute confidence," he said. "You'll understand why when I explain what this is about."

"All my clients, Mr. Petrosky, are assured of total confidentiality and care in how their situations are approached."

I had his name on the sheet Octavia had left for me, as well as the name of the person who had referred him. Octavia had looked that person up and left me a note regarding that case. She was priceless, was Octavia, and no less so because I knew the reason for her efficiency and she knew I knew: Octavia liked working for me because I left her ample scope to develop all her skills, legal and secretarial, and because she thought that without her I would get myself into a fine old tangle. I knew that men, at least in the old days, had had secretaries like this, but Octavia's devotion to me was a bit different. She wasn't acting like a wife; she wasn't half in love with me. She had simply decided to make sure I succeeded in my profession, and she kept her eyes on everything. I tried not to become dependent, but of course I did. Still, I told myself, I could manage without her. She, I was sure, told herself I could not manage without her. Somehow we had achieved a fine balance; I basked in her devotion, and she delighted in my success. And all this with both of us knowing that, in any relationship more personal than ours, we would not get along at all.

Mr. Petrosky settled back into his chair and I got out my notebook. "I'm glad that Mrs. Staunton recommended me," I said. "Please tell me how I can help you."

"It's really nice to see a young woman with some flesh on her," Mr. Petrosky said. "I hope you don't mind my mentioning it. I expect you make your clients feel comfortable; not like some of those half-starved women these days who make you want to give them a good meal."

"I do enjoy a good meal, Mr. Petrosky," I said encouragingly. "Now, about your case."

I had already guessed that Mr. Petrosky would turn out to be a good guy, a lovable fellow—I'd guessed that even before he mentioned admiring my shape—and I turned out to be right. He had started his own law firm many years ago, together with two other lawyers, and they had made a good thing of it. Recently, he and his partners had become amalgamated with a much larger firm, taken over in fact. Mr. Petrosky had made it part of the deal that his staff would stay with them in the new firm, and that had been satisfactorily arranged. The only people he really worried about were his secretary, one of his partner's secretaries—both of them longtime fixtures—and an associate who had never been made a partner but who was considered permanent and who had contributed a good deal to the practice. Here followed a long explanation of why this associate had not been made a partner, which Mr. Petrosky felt was a necessary piece of information for me to have. It wasn't really; I had already gathered the fact of his devotion to this associate.

The new firm, I learned as my new client got down to cases, wanted to fire this associate; they were accusing him of stealing from the firm to the tune of two or three hundred thousand dollars. "Which is ridiculous," Mr. Petrosky said. "Harry wouldn't steal. It's not in his nature. But they've got all sorts of evidence, stuff off computers and financial sheets, and what they call proof that it had to be him. They also claim that his bank account has deposits that are unusual. Don't ask me how they got to see his bank account. It seems that anyone can find out anything about anyone these days. Maybe it's the Internet."

"And you want me to look into it," I said encouragingly. I felt grateful to Mr. Petrosky. This was the kind of case I knew how to handle, and would handle well. True, should the associate turn out to have been fiddling with the books, it would not be easy to have to tell Mr. Petrosky so. My suspicion, however, was that the firm was using a not unusual sort of leverage to get the associate to quit. But why?

"There are two possibilities," I told my client. "Either your associate is up to new tricks or"—I held up my hand as he began to protest—"they do want to get rid of him. The question is, why would they want to get rid of him?"

"That's what I want you to find out for me. Mrs. Staunton said you were wonderful; she admired the way you went about solving her problem."

We discussed a few more points, I reminded him of my fee, which he happily agreed to, and he gave me a check for the down payment. I stood to escort Mr. Petrosky out of my office, opening the door for him, shaking the hand he held out to me, and telling him that we would be in touch as soon as I had information, even if it was of no progress. I saw Octavia beginning to take down more necessary information from him as I closed my door.

I put my feet up on my desk and settled back into my old, efficient, professional self. The hell with Clifton College and Professor Haycock. I couldn't imagine why I had ever agreed to get involved. Probably I thought it would be a new experience; maybe I thought I'd meet some interesting people, some problems different from the business and marital kind I was used to and, I reminded myself, good at.

Well, I had met interesting people, women especially. Maybe it was worth it to meet Antonia and Elaine Kimberly. Even Dawn was a bit different from the usual order of executive assistant. And of course Kate. Well, knowing when you're licked is a sign of professional competence. I got in over my head, and having treaded water for a while, I was now swimming to shore—shore being my office, Octavia, and Mr. Petrosky. I began to think about his case.

But of course, I reminded myself, I would have to tell Kate Fansler I was giving up. She'd been good at supporting me and not letting me get too morose about my failure, but this time she'd have to admit we would never know who had offed Professor Haycock. Then there was Don. Well, maybe one day I'd ride out, pick Don up at the station, and take him to our booth for a reunion beer. Maybe, but probably not. I felt bad about that, but I also realized the case was the glue in our friendship, and no glue, no sticking. It surprised me how relieved I felt. I'd send in a final bill, say the case was beyond solution, and tell Kate I was through.

I was just getting ready to do some research on the Internet for Mr. Petrosky—it's amazing what you can learn on the Web—when Octavia buzzed me. It was Kate Fansler. I'd always suspected the woman of being a mind reader.

"Hi," I said. "I was just going to call you."

"Oh," she said. "What about?"

"About how I'm giving up on Haycock and all those

who sail with him. I can't tell you what a relief it is. It takes a brave person to admit she's failed, to face the fact and sign off. Octavia is even now preparing their bill." That was not quite true, but she would be preparing it before too long.

"Well, tell her to hold off for a bit. Could you come by tonight? About eight?"

"Kate, I'd love to, but things have rather piled up here and—"

"It will be the last time, I promise. I hope you'll visit us again, but this will be the last time we shall mention Clifton College."

"Or Haycock, or Tennyson, or *Freshwater?*" I rather rudely asked.

"Absolutely," Kate said. "I may decide to quote from 'Maud' again on some distant occasion, but you won't have to take it personally."

"Good enough. I'll be there. Eight on the dot."

"I'd better warn you. We're going to watch a movie."

"A movie! Really, Kate, I'd far rather talk or walk with Banny or—"

"Trust me, Woody. And don't ride here on your motorcycle; you may want several drinks before the evening is finished."

Well, all right, academics are all peculiar; at least I'd learned that. Meanwhile, blessed Mr. Petrosky had reminded me who I was, what I was good at, and how I earned my living. I turned on the computer and got to work.

I took the subway to Kate's house. If she said I might want to drink, I had to believe I would want to. I had gotten in the way of trusting Kate; there was no doubt of that. At the same time, I knew I had to be firm about my decision to end my association with this case. I had appreciated her honesty on that nighttime walk in the park with Banny, when she told me the reasons I shouldn't quit, but no such argument was going to work this time. And we were to watch a movie. Well, I'd learned one thing: even the nicest of academics tends to act a bit odd from time to time.

Banny and Kate came to the door to greet me. They led me into the living room; then Kate told me to have a seat, and offered a drink. I accepted, but with some uncomfortable qualms. It was clear Kate had something up her sleeve. Nothing I could do but sit back and let whatever it was happen.

Kate, however, seemed determined to chat, and I decided the hell with that. "If we have to see a movie, let's see it," I said. "Who's in it, anyway?"

"Everybody, or so it seems," Kate said. "Wendy Hiller, Ingrid Bergman, Anthony Perkins, Albert Finney, Sean Connery, Vanessa Redgrave, John Gielgud—that's just for starters. I can't remember who else, but they're all famous, even to an old-timer like me."

"All in one movie?" I was beginning to worry about Kate's sanity.

"Absolutely. Shall we watch it now?"

"Absolutely," I said. "What's it called?"

"Murder on the Orient Express," Kate said.

It sounded vaguely familiar, but I couldn't quite remember it or what it was about. "What's the date on it?" I asked.

"1974," Kate said.

I would have been eight or nine, I thought. Maybe I'd gone to it with my mom. If so, it had vanished out of memory. It seemed likelier that I hadn't seen it, however. My mom didn't like movies with murders in them, let alone *murder* in the title. Mom has given up on movies altogether these days. As far as she was concerned, they stopped making good movies when Fred Astaire quit. Now I was investigating murders, but I didn't see many movies either. It just didn't seem to fit into my way of life. Not that I can't work a VCR. I live alone and like to watch movies there from time to time. But movie theatres, no.

Kate stuck the film into the VCR and pushed PLAY on the remote. I was glad to see she could manage that. I've noticed that most people over fifty have trouble with VCRs unless they're particularly handy types.

They say if you want to use a VCR you ought to have a six-year-old in the house. I knew people who couldn't watch movies on video once their kids left home. I didn't usually get asked to showings at other people's houses, and I couldn't help wondering what the hell was on Kate's mind.

I took a sip of my drink and sat back to watch, feeling rather the way I did when I visited my family. One did what they wanted to do, and movies, or the soaps, were better than the same old conversations, not that you could call them conversations.

It was an old tape, and groaned a little; the sound was not great. It opened with a 1930 scene about a kidnapping and murder of a little girl—very spotty and old-fashioned. Then we were in Istanbul five years later.

I'd gathered by now that this was an Agatha Christie job. I asked Kate when it had been written. She said in 1934. So we were being contemporary with old Agatha.

Watching, I slowly came to the sad conclusion that Kate had gone ballistic. We met the characters one at a time—two, if they were in love—all getting on the same damn train. Nice train, though. I liked those old trains with the steam and wheels, although some poor mug had to shovel coal to keep it going. We met Poirot, played by someone all wrong, in my opinion. I haven't read much Christie that I can remember, but I have seen David Suchet, and he was my idea of Poirot. This guy looked like he was putting on an act and trying to appear small, which he wasn't. Well, it turns out there's a bad guy—we know that because he won't let his secretary finish his soup, let alone the rest of the meal—and he ends up dead, drugged and stabbed lots of times. Everybody was made up to look aged and peculiar. I mean, I saw Wendy Hiller not long ago in one of the P. D. James mysteries on TV, and she looked older here than she did twenty-five years later. As for Ingrid Bergman . . . Well, never mind. Poirot interviewed them all one at a time, and seemed to me to be getting nowhere fast.

Why was Kate making us watch this creaking old mess with everybody in it famous? None of Poirot's questions, let alone the answers, seemed to make any sense at all. He kept gathering facts and impressions, and none of them showed any sign of leading anywhere. Like me. I began to watch the movie a bit more closely, or anyway, less resentfully.

That this was all connected to the kidnapping we'd seen at the beginning was becoming clear. So far only one or two of the characters had admitted knowing the family of the kidnapped girl, but that was the way the wind was blowing—it all had to do with that crime, which had resulted, we learned, in the deaths of four other people besides: the kid's father and mother, an accused housemaid who hanged herself because wrongly accused—I ask you—and, well there must have been one other, but at the moment I forget who.

Poirot solved it, of course. If you don't know the end, I'm sorry to spoil it for you, but the movie's so creaky you probably want to give it a miss. It turns out that everyone has lied, but Poirot knew the truth behind their lies, arrived at by reasoning I thought a bit far-fetched. Detective story writers: they all make these leaps, which I could hardly do. What would Mr. Petrosky think if I summoned everyone before me and told them they were liars, but the truth was . . .

It turned out that they had all done it—planned it and done it together. They were all connected to the kidnapping and the household at that time. So they had drugged the mean guy and then each of them had plunged a dagger into him. Naturally, there turned out to be a convenient doctor in the Calais coach who could tell human from animal blood just by looking at it, and there turned out to be a snowstorm holding up the train so everything could be solved before they left the place where they were stuck. It all got enacted in replay before our eyes as Poirot explained it. No need to provide proof or anything like that. And then they decided to withhold everything and let the stupid police in the next town, in the Balkans of all places, assume the murderer escaped. I ask you. Everybody clicked glasses of champagne and all was well. Whoopie-do.

"Well, Kate," I said as we reached the end of this riveting entertainment, "thank you for sharing that with me. I must say detective work was a lot easier in those days, at least in films."

"Did you find it unrealistic?" she said.

"I wouldn't go that far," I said, allowing myself the relief of sarcasm. "But of all the preposterous, unlikely, stupid stories, this one takes the cake. And even if that was how the murder was done, there was no way Poirot could possibly have guessed it. To say nothing of the fact that for no reason offered he seemed to have total recall of the five-year-old kidnapping that happened in a country he'd never even visited. Why should he have been able to solve anything as unsolvable as that crazy murder . . . ?"

And then I got it. Okay, I was pretty slow about getting it, but who am I to identify with Poirot and a movie supposedly set in Yugoslavia over a quarter of a century ago? Of course, I might have asked myself why Kate wanted me to watch this creaky old thing, and not just sit there assuming she was just another flaky academic.

"You think they all did it?" I said, holding out my glass.

Kate took it from me, fixed both of us new drinks, and sat down.

"It's a guess," Kate said. "No more than that. I don't

know what made me think of the book in connection with Clifton College—I thought of the book first, by the way. It was originally called *Murder in the Calais Coach*. Anyway, Reed happened to wonder if anyone read Agatha Christie anymore, and I said I thought so. It occurred to me to look at one of her mysteries just to see how it would strike me now. I hadn't read her for ages. We had a few of her books, but it must have been my subconscious or dumb luck that made me pick this one. I read it, and was going to suggest you read it, when it seemed to me the film, which I did vaguely remember, would concentrate our attention better. End of story."

She sipped her drink and then said, "Let's go over all you know. Not out loud, but in our minds. After you've had a think, let me know if there is any reason this couldn't have been a crime like Christie's, with pills, of course, rather than a dagger."

"There is one thing," I said. "I never paid much attention to it before, but everyone kept talking about how horrible retsina tasted. I'll have to go back and ask, but my impression is that much was made of its horrible taste, and the bottle may have just stood there a while, or been passed around as they discussed it."

"Exactly," Kate said. "My guess is that they wanted to make sure that anyone wanting to take a taste would do it before the pills got into the bottle. Not that there were many there who didn't know what was happening, but they didn't take any chances."

"You're saying that every person I questioned led me around by the nose, knowing all along they'd been one of the pill droppers?"

"Not quite everyone. But most of them. They were very clever in seeming to confide in you and earn your sympathy, while not giving you any useful information."

"They even tried to hide the fact that ex-dean Elaine Kimberly had been there. I suppose her coming to the party seemed a bit odd; she must have felt a strong reason to take part, to take the risk with the others."

"I don't think the students were involved. Do you?"

"Well, why did Oakwood get one of his student groupies to substitute for the girl who was supposed to be there?" I was asking questions not for the answers, but to try to get my mind in some kind of order.

"A precaution, don't you think? If the groupie noticed anything, he would be in a position to hear about it, and to distract her. Something like that."

I was thinking it all through. "And the reason Oakwood beat up Petrillo. The poor guy, who's a good Catholic and a very upright person, may have been cracking. He may have said something to Oakwood about giving themselves up, admitting it all, whatever. That's probably why Oakwood jumped him."

"Doubtless their motives differed. As in the movie.

They each probably feared and despised Haycock for his or her own reason. At the same time, they must have felt they were saving the department and the college from a terrible outcome."

I just nodded, going over in my mind everything I had learned, everything Don had learned. It fit. It goddamn fit. Kate had been right that they had hired me because I might not be able to solve the crime. She had been right that Claire Wiseman guessed that and wanted to keep me from being set up. But I'd sure as hell been set up. I could feel anger beginning to rise in me like a geyser. Like Old Faithful at Yellowstone, bursting out with steam and hot air. I hate being a patsy. I don't mind failing, but I hate being made a patsy.

I said that to Kate. I wondered how she was going to find comfort in this situation. As far as I was concerned at that moment, I would gladly have gotten them all in a room and told them what happened, like Poirot in the film. Just to let them know I'd caught on. Just to let them know they hadn't fooled me.

"You told me about all your conversations in some detail," Kate said, "and my impression, which I do not say to make you feel better—it's the absolute truth—is that they all came to like you, even to trust you—well, maybe not Oakwood, but most of the others—and they were as honest with you as they could be, more honest than they would have been with anyone else. You have a right to feel angry, but you'd be wrong to think they were glad to be fooling you. One thing about a group murder is that you have to consider the safety of everyone who was in it with you."

"You think Petrillo would have talked?"

"Probably not. My guess is that he was trying it out on someone. He picked the wrong guy."

I was quieting down a bit—anyway, seething less.

"What are we going to do?" I asked Kate.

"It's your decision. It's what you're going to do that you have to decide. But I did mention this solution to Reed and he doubted whether anyone, let alone the New Jersey police, could get a conviction. They might even have trouble with the grand jury. There's no evidence. A good lawyer, and the college would surely hire one if they haven't already got him or her on retainer, would make mincemeat of this story. That is just a fact to put in the hopper with other facts when you try to decide what to do."

"Okay," I said. "What would you do? And don't tell me it's my decision; I know that. I'm asking what you would do."

"I think I'd just let it go. But after all, I am an academic, and what I would do has to be different from what you would do."

"And nobody hung you out to dry," I said.

"I think that's putting it a bit strongly, but you're

right. I'm not the one on the spot, as you have pointed out. On the other hand, you're a professional private investigator. Sometimes you fail to bring a case to conclusion. That must happen to all detectives, private or police, certainly to the FBI and the CIA. You write a sensible report, send a large bill, take the money, and run. You have the satisfaction of having guessed what happened, and that should count for something."

I realized I was feeling a bit better. Kate got us each another drink, but I noticed, as I had before in times of extreme stress, that liquor didn't seem to have any effect on me. Still, I was a bit looser, from what Kate had said more than from the hooch.

"I have a Jewish friend," I told her, "who's got a joke about a religious Jew who sneaks off to play golf on Yom Kippur. He hits a hole in one. And he can't tell anyone. That's my situation. If I decide to do nothing, I suppose I can't even tell Octavia. No one knows but you and Reed. I assume I don't have to tell Claire Wiseman."

"I don't see why you should tell her, if you want to let the whole thing go, as Poirot did in the movie. But you can't decide now. Why don't you think about it for a few days? There's no real rush."

"True," I said, getting up. Banny's tail thumped. What I didn't ask was, What about Don Jackson? What the hell was I going to do about him? I felt I owed him honesty, yet how well did I know him; how much could I trust him?

I took a taxi back to Brooklyn, and actually fell asleep the minute after I got home and threw myself on the bed. I realized I hadn't turned on my cell phone, and I didn't. Everything—if there was anything, even Mr. Petrosky—could wait.

CHAPTER FOURTEEN

And I would that my tongue could utter
The thoughts that arise in me.
　　　　—Tennyson, "Break, Break, Break"

I slept far into the morning, until Octavia woke me by letting the phone ring a hundred times. She said she had been about to call the police, but had decided to come herself first if I didn't answer. I apologized as best I could, and said I would be there within the hour. I took a long shower, letting the water run through my hair and into my mouth. Then of course I had to blow-dry my hair, get myself and my clothes together, drink some juice and coffee, and let the day begin.

On the way to my office, I allowed myself to relish the relief I felt at having this damn case over. I hadn't realized it, or let myself realize it, but the sense of failure and frustration had been wearing away at me. Now I knew what had happened, the fact that no one else besides Kate and Reed might know didn't matter all that much. I could stop thinking of myself as incompetent and unable to solve anything but ordinary, crass crimes. Of course I wanted to shout it to the world, to burst in upon the dean and tell him what had happened; I wanted to dare him to do something about it. I wanted to be redeemed; I wanted to be praised and told that I did as well as anybody could have; I wanted my pride in my work restored to me.

But, I told myself, my pride had been restored. Not publicly, not in the eyes of everyone connected with Haycock and Clifton College, but inside me, where it mattered, and in Kate's eyes. There was no doubt that some things needed to be kept secret. I rode across the Queensborough Bridge feeling like it was the beginning of a new life. "Here I come, Mr. Petrosky," I sang, to no particular tune. My voice was drowned out by my bike and other traffic noise.

When I got to the office Octavia looked at me in a distinctly worried way, but I told her all was well, to send the final account off to the people in the English department at Clifton College, marking it *Case Closed.*

"It's going to be a pretty stiff bill," she said. "You put in a lot of hours, though the expenses are lower than usual."

"If they object, we'll decide how to argue then. Somehow I think they'll just pay it." Feeling satisfied, I thought to myself that they'd done the right thing in hiring a private investigator, and had gotten away with Haycock's demise exactly as they had hoped they would.

"Professor Kate Fansler called," Octavia said. "She said would you call her back when you get in."

"Fine. Then I'm off on the Petrosky case."

"Glad we're on to something else," Octavia said. Sometimes I wonder how much Octavia figures out on her own. I made up my mind long ago that I would never ask her.

Back in my office I rang up Kate.

"I'm glad to hear from you," she said. "I hoped you'd be hugely relieved to have that academic caper behind you, but I wanted to hear from your own lips that you were. Or not."

"Definitely relieved," I said. "And I find I'm taking a lot of credit for solving the thing, even though it was you and Poirot who played a significant part in the solution. But if I hadn't gotten it from that creaky film, or had denied that what the film suggested could be the solution, you wouldn't have pressed it, would you?" I'd been wondering about that.

"No," Kate said. "Definitely not."

"So in a way I solved it. I got to the edge and you just gave me a little shove."

"Exactly. Last evening, or anyway when I told Reed about it, I recalled a story I heard long ago, and I have waited many years for the applicable moment to tell it. I think this is that moment. Can you bear to hear it? Have you the time?"

"I'm listening," I said. I felt as though suddenly I had all the time in the world.

"It's about a man—stories were always about men in those days—who was standing on the edge of a precipice admiring the view of the sunset and night coming on, when his footing gave way. Tumbling down and down the mountainside, he finally managed to catch hold of the branch of a bush. He held on as long as he could, dangling from one arm. Finally his grip simply gave way, and he had to let go. He fell six inches to the ground."

"Nice story," I said.

"Almost as good as your story about the Jewish golf player."

"Let's call it a tie," I said. "But you know, Kate, it's a funny thing how little Tennyson turned out to have to do with all this. He was a symptom of Haycock's problems, but not really a clue."

"Funny you should mention that," Kate said. "I've just started reading a new book about Auden, incidentally by another academic,* and I came across Auden saying about Tennyson—hold on, here it is—that Tennyson *'was* the Victorian mouthpiece in *In Memoriam* when he was thinking of his grief. When he decided to

*Edward Mendelson, *Later Auden* (New York: Farrar, Straus and Giroux, 1999), p.18.

be the Victorian bard and wrote *Idylls of the King*, he ceased to be a poet.' I think the same must have been true of Haycock. He was a real academic when he began with Tennyson. Then he tried to become *the* academic and *the* Tennysonian, and ceased to be even a decent professor."

"Interesting," I said. And true, no doubt. But, I said to myself, at the same time, if no one ever mentioned Tennyson again, except maybe Kate quoting 'Maud,' it would be quite all right with me.

Kate seemed to guess my thought. "Come and see me sometime, Woody," she said. "I promise not to inflict any literary silliness on you."

"Right," I said. "And I'll need to remind you that in me you have your only fat friend, and your only friend who rides a motorbike."

"I don't need to be reminded about you," Kate said. "I'll call you in a month or so."

And being Kate, she would, I thought. It wasn't just an empty promise, as it would have been with most folks. I was glad I'd met Kate Fansler, and I meant to see her again.

Meanwhile, I had to make up my mind about Don Jackson. I still didn't know if I wanted to tell him the outcome of our case or not, but I had at least to let him know it was over as far as I was concerned. And I had to say goodbye. Without taking too much time to think, I called Don's cell phone and got him.

"How goes it, Woody?" he said.

"Just great, Don. I've decided the case is over. The police can grind away if they want to, but I don't think we'll get any nearer to a solution if we keep going around in circles for the next six years." That was true in a literal sense, even if it was cutting it a little close. Still, it wasn't a lie.

"You coming out to New Jersey to drink to the end of the case?" Don asked. "I rather think the police will go along with your decision, whether they exactly say so or not. They're mighty handy at keeping cases open without doing anything about them."

"I don't think I want to go anywhere near Clifton College ever again," I told Don. "I'll send them a formal report and a final accounting. But I would like to have that end-of-case beer. Is there anywhere else in New Jersey we could meet, maybe near one of the tunnels?"

"I'll come to New York," Don said. "I'll even come to Brooklyn. You say where, and I'll meet you there for beer and whatever else, say at six-thirty. How's that?"

For a moment I thought of asking him up to my place. We could bring in beer and a pizza and just sit around. But I soon thought better of it. He was bound to think it meant something significant, and then he would have to deal with that. And however he dealt with it, it wouldn't make for a pleasant, casual time. So I told him about a pretty nice bar I knew, with booths, not great or anything, but comfortable. No need for him to go all the way to Brooklyn.

"Not a New York fancy place?" he asked.

"Not a bit." I gave him the address. I was about to tell him how to find it when I remembered he'd lived in New York a lot longer than in New Jersey, and didn't need directions.

So that was settled. I still hadn't made up my mind whether to tell him the truth about the Haycock case or not; I planned to leave that decision to work itself out with the beer. I thought that, after talking with him again for a while, I'd know whether I wanted to level with him or not, which meant whether to trust him or not. Which meant a lot of things.

I got to the bar a little early, thinking I'd grab us a booth and wait for him, but Don was there ahead of me, already in a booth and almost at the end of his first beer. He got up to greet me, and then I slid into my side of the booth across from him.

"You relieved?" he asked.

"You'd better believe it. I feel fifty pounds lighter," I said, and then laughed. "Not literally, of course." For some reason I felt embarrassed, and annoyed at myself for saying that. He didn't take any notice.

"Me too," Don said. "I suppose if we worked on each of the people at that party for a year or so, someone might tell us something about what he or she knew, might give us some idea of who did it, but I have to ask myself, Is it worth it? And I answer myself: No, it isn't. The hell with it."

"A very immoral, illegal conclusion," I said.

"Very. But hell, many murders go unsolved, including a number I've heard of that needed to be solved a lot more than this one does."

"Too true," I said.

We ordered hamburgers, cheeseburgers actually, and they came with French fries and coleslaw. We each had another beer. I liked eating with Don because he liked eating. He didn't need to act like food didn't really matter to him, and he didn't work at it as though it was the main reason for our being there. Well, it was true, he ate and did a lot of other things just right.

We didn't talk about the case. It was over for us, and nothing was to be gained by tossing it around. I asked Don if he still liked working with the police force in that college town, and he said he did, on the whole. There were some okay guys and some crappers, but it was a good life. His kids were coming soon during some week off the teachers took at their school for conferences or something. Don was looking forward to their visit, and had some plans laid out.

"What about you?" he asked.

"I've got a few cases ongoing," I said, "and a new one that looks promising. It's right up my alley, not something full of Tennyson and *Freshwater*."

"Freshwater?"

"I probably mentioned it in passing," I said. "A play the professors in the English department put on, to the great discomfort of Haycock. It wasn't really important. No wonder you forgot it." I thought that I would have forgotten it too, if Kate hadn't gone on about it so.

We finished our hamburgers, and decided not to have anything else to eat, just a final beer. We didn't say much drinking it. Not that we felt uneasy sitting there, or uncomfortable with each other. We just didn't have anything worth saying at that moment, and found the silence comfortable, both of us thinking our thoughts.

I knew by then that I wouldn't tell Don about how the murder really was committed. What was the point? I'd have to swear him to secrecy, and that would be a burden for him. If the case had been ongoing, I'd have had to tell him anything I found out, but since it was over, let it be over. It wasn't that I couldn't trust him. It was that there was no decent reason to burden him with that trust.

I smiled at him, and he smiled back. When we got up to leave—I paid; I said it was my turf, and he'd paid for our first meal in New Jersey—he didn't argue. He just said, "Thanks, Woody."

We drove to Penn Station on my bike with him on the back. He held on to me, with his arms around my waist. When he got off, he waved, and I waved and watched him walk into the station. Then he was gone, and I was on my way back to Brooklyn and my own life.